I0745807

BAD KING

M. MALONE

Print ISBN: 978-1-938789-48-9

Ebook ISBN: 978-1-938789-39-7

Contents

Also by M. Malone

BEG ME (Milo & Mya)

My rooster is on strike. Yeah, I can't believe it either. But he'll only crow for one woman. Spoiler Alert *she hates me*

ASK ME (Andre & Casey)

Am I arrogant? Maybe. Do women still want me? Abso-F'ing-lutely. Then I meet the one woman who isn't impressed.

NEED ME (Vin & Ariana)

Crazy sh*t every day keeps relationships away. Except there's one guy who just *keeps* showing up. And if I'm not careful, I might get used to needing someone.

WANT ME (Law & Anya)

No strings attached. Sounds good, right? Except if I'm not her boyfriend ... the position is open for someone else.

*** Join my VIP list for FREE books ***

newsletter.mmalonebooks.com

- Contemporary Romance -

Blue-Collar Billionaires

Billions from the deadbeat dad they never knew sounds pretty sweet.
Until they find out what he really wants.

Tank / Finn / Gabe / Zack / Luke

The Alexanders

One More Day : "Good girl" Ridley has always attracted bad guys. Now she's on the run and has nowhere to hide. So when Jackson Alexander mistakes her for her twin, she decides to do something she knows is wrong. *She lies.*

The Things I Do for You : Nicholas Alexander finally has something the woman of his dreams needs. He'll give Raina a baby if she gives him what he wants. *Her.*

He's the Man : Matt Simmons is over Army doctors poking him until he sees his old babysitter, now a physical therapist, is h-o-t. Suddenly he's seeing the benefits of therapy.

All I Want: The only thing Kaylee wants is for Elliott Alexander to stop treating her like she's invisible. But a car accident forces her to reach out to the only man she trusts to save her.

All I Need is You : When the man she loves leaves town after their steamy kiss, Kaylee Wilhelm is done. But when she's targeted by a stalker, Eli is the only one who can protect her.

Say You Will : Mara Simmons has always known Trent Townsend is *The One*. But when she suspects his frequent business trips have *nothing* to do with business, she sets in motion a chain of events bigger than she can imagine and discovers that the man she loves just might be a stranger.

Just One Thing : Scientist Bennett Alexander is a bona fide genius but he still can't figure out how to "get the girl". So he hires a dating tutor. What could go wrong? Other than falling for his teacher, of course.

Bad King: My parents just put a gold diggers target on my back. But if all they want is a wedding, I can do that. I'll find the fiancee of their nightmares. *Who Wants to Marry a Billionaire? Must be completely inappropriate.*

Bad Blood : I'd do anything for my best friend's little sister. Until she asks for the one thing I can't give. One night. No rules. ***2019 RITA® Award Winner!***

- Romantic Suspense -

(Co-authored with Nana Malone)

- The Shameless Trilogy
- The Force Duet
- The Deep Duet
- The Sin Duet

- The Brazen Duet

- Paranormal Romance -

Nathan's Heart

The Brotherhood of Bandits

BAD KING

____

Chapter 1

____

Olivia Reyes shifted from foot to foot, trying not to lose her balance while balancing her cell phone between her shoulder and her ear. After listening to the phone ring, she immediately hung up and called back. Her best friend was notorious for disappearing into his work at all hours but it wasn't like him not to answer her texts.

Just before she was about to hang up again, he answered with a distracted "Hello."

"Finally! I've been calling and calling. I was about to send out a search party."

"Oh, hey Boo."

She wrinkled her nose at the nickname. "How many years have to pass before you stop calling me that?"

He chuckled as she knew he would. "It's instinct now. I will forever associate peek-a-boo with my Olivia."

"Whatever. I've been trying to reach you. What's up with you ignoring my texts?"

"Sorry. I really meant to call you last night but I'm in the middle of testing the newest iteration of my soil. I started reading my notes from the last phase of testing."

"Of course. The last time we spoke you'd decided to alter the nitrogen levels again, right?"

She smiled to herself as his voice became more and more animated as he explained the changes he was making. Bennett Alexander was probably the only person in the world who could wax poetic about the mineral levels in dirt. She could just picture him in his home lab, probably wearing jeans and one of those hideous sweaters with his glasses pushed up on top of his head. It was a sweet image that never failed to make her smile.

Despite the fact that he was a genius and she was ... not, he loved to tell her about his work. And she genuinely loved hearing about it. He was awkward, always had been, but after growing up together they had a unique way of communicating that probably didn't make sense to anyone else. He always made her feel like he valued her opinion.

Even if she never had any clue what he was talking about.

"You sound really excited, Ben. I hope this new batch is the one."

He made a distracted noise. "It has to be. The changing weather patterns have really messed with our crops in recent years. We need soil that's robust enough to gain us maximum yield this coming summer."

When he started mumbling to himself she figured she'd better get to the point of the call before she lost him again.

"Bennett? Hey!"

"Sorry. I'm still here."

"Your mom said you've been nominated for a Mentor Science award! That's awesome."

After more mumbling and what sounded like a curse, he finally responded again.

"Yes, I just got the invitation to the awards ceremony. Wait, you talked to my mom?"

She smothered a laugh. "Well, you weren't answering your phone as usual. So I figured Julia could at least make sure you were still breathing!"

"Great. So that's why she put the invitation out for me to see. I was wondering why she bothered. Social gatherings have never been my favorite thing."

"Um, well she did that because I asked her to. I was hoping that you'd take me as your date."

On the other end of the line, it got quiet. Too quiet.

"I was just thinking that we don't get to spend nearly enough time together these days, you know? And I can talk to everyone for you when you get nervous."

Olivia knew she was babbling but considering how easily Bennett got freaked out, it was better than letting the awful silence continue.

"That's true. I'm no good at this kind of stuff but you always cover for me." Bennett sounded confused.

Poor guy. She hadn't hit on him since their disastrous first kiss the same summer he got his braces taken off. But after a few years of dating duds it was time for her to get serious. Bad boys were hot but they weren't the type you made a family with. And that's something she hadn't had in a long time.

"I don't mind covering for you, you know that. So, it's a date! I'll call you later. Bye!"

She hung up quickly before he had a chance to respond. No doubt he had no clue what had just happened. Bennett was brilliant in math and science but socially, not so much. She'd seen many times that any interaction with the opposite sex was enough to send him into a stammering, blushing frenzy.

The only reason he could function around her was he'd known her so long that she didn't think he really saw her as a woman. But she just knew that if they gave it a chance they could make it work. He was gorgeous, freakishly smart and he already loved her.

What the hell more did she need?

Passion. Excitement. Desire. Remember those things?

The door to her office opened and Imogen stuck her head around the door. "Boss lady? The member and his guests have arrived. Dita and I have set up everything per the client profile."

"Thank you, Gen. I'll be out in just a moment."

After the door shut behind her, the music stopped abruptly. Having a soundproof office was a blessing most days but perhaps if she could have heard the music she wouldn't have wasted so much time daydreaming. Instead she'd been standing here for the past ten minutes lamenting the fact that she might never get laid again. At least, not with anyone she was really attracted to.

She shook off the negative thoughts and quickly attached the last garter on the mid-thigh slip she wore. An elegant champagne lace with a deep plunge V-neck, it was the kind of thing a wife would wear when she wanted to seduce her husband. That was tonight's member request, a boudoir theme.

After shrugging into the matching satin robe, she picked up the information card she'd printed in advance of tonight's bachelor party. When she saw the client code she groaned.

It was King.

Olivia treated all of the members of Club VIP with polite detachment. They were paying exorbitant membership fees and by extension, financing an extremely comfortable life for her and her partners. But Thane Kingsley was the most infuriating, arrogant, high-handed man she'd ever met. It took all of her restraint sometimes to hold her tongue.

And he definitely knew it. She'd swear the man only came back so often to drive her insane.

Well, whatever. All the girls who worked in her section of Club VIP knew to review the member's requests prior to setting up the room so she wasn't worried. Imogen was a little rough around the edges but she was professional at least.

His Royal Highness, as she referred to him behind his back, would have no reason to complain about the service. He'd had *the nerve* to complain about the way the room was set up during his first month of membership and while Olivia had been perfectly polite, she had no doubt she'd scared him a little with her icy cold response.

She was getting fired up again just thinking about it. Who the hell did he think he was? The only reason the set up hadn't been to his liking was because he hadn't filled out his preference list completely. The Masquerade Room was the epitome of wish fulfillment and every detail was customized to the client's preferences.

Her dream had been a place where high profile people could find their fantasy without exposure or risk of being recognized. After moving in that world of the rich and wealthy once, she thought she understood their needs better than most.

Her family hadn't been anywhere near as wealthy as her friend Elle, no yachts or chauffeurs, but as the only daughter of a successful Virginia horse rancher, she'd never wanted for anything. Their ranch adjoined the Alexander homestead on one side which was how she knew Bennett. It had been a good life before it all fell apart.

She put a hand over her now flat belly. Things were going to be fine. After a few years of co-owning the club, she was almost financially independent at last and it wasn't like she was going to do this forever. She'd move on, hopefully get married to Bennett and start having little Einstein babies who were just as amazing as their father. He never had to know about Club VIP.

If Bennett ever found out about her new career, how far she'd fallen, he'd be disappointed or even disgusted. But it'd be even worse if he ever guessed her most secret shame.

That she loved every minute of it.

"Okay, let's do this."

She picked up the black satin eye mask on her desk and slid it firmly in place. It was time to show this bachelor party why they were the most exclusive pleasure club on the East Coast. Thane Kingsley might be the bane of her existence but this party wasn't for him, it was a bachelor party for a friend.

The man of the hour might have crappy taste in friends but he still deserved a fantastic sendoff.

When she opened the door leading to the main room, the deep, hypnotic throb of the music hit her like a wave. The bachelor party was already seated on the low-slung couches peppered around the room. Ten pairs of eyes swung her way, all of them assessing.

Wanting.

Instantly warmth curled in her belly. King's eyes met hers and she squared her shoulders, ignoring the little throb in her lower belly.

"Gentlemen, my name is Angel. Welcome to the Masquerade room."

Chapter 2

King sat back on the surprisingly comfortable couch and watched as one of the top executives of his company enjoyed a lap dance.

His best friend, James Hamilton III, leaned over, his voice raising to carry over the driving beat of the music.

"It was good of you to host the bachelor party for Devin. I don't think the poor bastard actually has any other friends." The entire time, James' eyes stayed on the dancer gyrating against Devin's lap.

"That's because he's in the office twenty hours out of the day. Just like the rest of us." King tugged at the knot of his tie. They'd all come directly from the office in fact.

James shrugged. "Still, it was nice of you. None of us have

the connections to score a membership to Club VIP. I heard they grant less than ten access keys per year."

King knew that to be accurate because he'd had to pay a hefty sum to get them to bend the rules and allow his membership. In the end he'd gotten what he wanted, as usual.

There wasn't much that the Kingsley name and money couldn't buy.

"Well, I figured it was the least I could do. After all, he's already fucked. Poor bastard actually thinks he's in love."

James grunted. "On that note, Harris already started the divorce pool. My money is on the six-month mark."

"You actually think they'll get that far?"

"Have you seen his fiancée? I'm pretty sure he'll put up with whatever crazy shit she does for a while just so he can continue to tap that on a regular basis."

King shook his head, completely bewildered by the idea of willingly shackling yourself to one woman. "I have no idea what is in the water lately but my executives are dropping like flies. Stanton got married last year, Stiles is up next and I just heard that Rollins is proposing to his girl soon."

"Face it, we're getting old." His friend's smile was bright even in the dark room.

Since King was a few years older, he figured the "getting old" quip was meant for him.

"Thirty-one isn't old. I wouldn't even be considering marriage if it wasn't for my parents shoving every gold digger over the legal age at me every time I go home."

"Yeah, I know all about those."

Uncomfortable, King looked around the room. James had defied his family a few years ago marrying his college girlfriend despite his parents' disapproval. His wife hadn't even waited until the ink was dry on the marriage certificate before she tried to empty his bank account. Ever since he seemed to have accepted that his fate was a loveless marriage.

"Sheila was a bitch, man. But that doesn't mean you have to get married to whatever plastic mannequin your parents push in front of you."

James shrugged. "I'm not doing it until I'm ready but I'm not fooling myself anymore. I want a family someday. So I'll eventually have to seal the deal with someone."

"Or you could stay single forever like me."

He was expecting his friend to laugh but an uncharacteristically somber expression crossed James' face.

"Don't push too hard, King. I regret so many things now. Fuck." He ran his hands through his dirty blond hair, disordering the slicked back strands. "If I had just listened when my father tried to warn me... whatever, it doesn't even matter now. Just think about it, okay?"

"I hear you but I can't live like this. My father actually threatened to hand over the reigns of Kingsley International to Colin. Can you imagine?"

"Not really. He hasn't gotten up before noon since he was in school."

"Exactly. He's still out partying every night and bringing home random chicks. I have worked too hard to lose it all now. I've given everything to this company."

"That's why you have to play the game. You have too much to lose now. Is pride really worth losing everything? Just marry someone they like, set her up with whatever she wants and then go have your fun on the side."

King rolled his eyes. "Interestingly enough, that is something my father would approve of whole-heartedly. But I don't like playing games."

"It's the American way." James leaned forward suddenly. "Oh, look at her. *Damn.*"

King stopped too, his eyes riveted on the young woman who had just entered the room.

Angel.

She was tall with a long fall of dark hair that spilled over her shoulders like a curtain. The creamy slip of lace she was wearing highlighted the honey tone of her skin and the lush curves of her breasts and hips. Despite the deep cut of the garment there was something elegant about it.

About her.

What the outfit also concealed was that she was about as cuddly as a porcupine. He'd made the mistake of offering a few minor suggestions on the way this section of the club was decorated and she'd almost sliced him open with that sharp tongue of hers.

Okay, he might have been a little overbearing in the beginning but was that any reason to take a guy's head off?

She was so... aggressive. That was totally not his type.

Except, ever since he'd started coming here he'd been having these fantasies about her. He wasn't even sure he liked her but damn if he didn't want to see what else that brash little mouth of hers could do. He could barely work in his home office anymore because he'd had so many fantasies about bending her over the surface.

But that was a fantasy that could never come true.

He might come out to Club VIP to play but he could just imagine his father's reaction if he was seen out with a stripper. The scandal would probably send him into an early grave.

Or scare him enough to take his nose out of King's business.

"Maybe I should play along," he murmured.

"What? Play with what?" James didn't take his eyes off Angel as she crossed the room, touching the shoulders of each of the men as she passed.

"With my father's games. If he wants me to get married so badly then I'll find a bride. In fact, I think I know just the woman for the job."

Chapter 3

Olivia watched as Imogen leaned down to hand the bachelor of the night a drink before planting herself in his lap. He stared up at her in awe and whispered something.

Imogen slipped a finger under the knot in his tie and pulled it off slowly. "Just sit back, sugar. I'm going to take care of everything," she crooned.

The young man looked up at her with his mouth open, clearly in awe. Olivia had to admit that in full costume, Gen was a sight to behold. With her big blue eyes and dusky coloring, she had the kind of beauty that often made men forget their vows, their values and even their names.

Little did they know that striking face hid a razor sharp intellect and instincts honed from a life on the street. Gen could probably take any man here in a bare-knuckle brawl.

Olivia smiled to herself. The men who came here had no idea what any of the dancers were really like. VIP was all about fantasy, after all.

It was the one thing she and the other partners drilled into their employees. Their members paid for an experience not skin. They could see girls in thongs anywhere. Here they got a full sensory experience in a safe, consensual environment.

She'd worked in several clubs doing things that kept her up at night and she'd sworn one day things would be different. Her girls were allowed to do what they were comfortable with as long as they focused on giving the members elegance paired with eroticism.

Sensuality was a beautiful thing and Olivia felt strongly that it should always be treated as such.

Dita, her newest hire, was on stage performing a beautiful contemporary dance routine. Her classical training was evident as was her discomfort with being topless. She'd styled her long blond hair so that it draped over her bare breasts and between moves she kept swiping at it, as if trying to keep it in place.

After working with her for the past three weeks, she was a lot better than when she first showed up. Even though Olivia's initial instinct was not to hire her, something about her was familiar. Truthfully, she reminded Olivia of a younger version of herself.

Inhibited, shy and drowning under the weight of others' disapproval.

She'd decided to give her a shot because she'd have never gotten anywhere if someone hadn't extended the same hand to her. Plus, it was a challenge. She wondered if one day the same things that mortified Dita now would one day fuel her. If she'd come to crave the attention and the empowerment of owning her sexuality and flaunting it.

While Dita danced, Olivia weaved her way through the gentlemen with a touch on the shoulder here and a brush against the cheek there. Their eyes followed her movements and she added a bit more swing to her step. Although she kept her eyes demurely lowered, all of her attention was on the dark-haired man in the back of the group.

King.

He'd been watching her with intense blue eyes ever since she walked in the room.

Adrenaline stormed through her system, so heady she almost swayed on her heels. His attention was powerful, a drug that made her want to keep the hits coming. She loved it and hated it at the same time.

When Dita finished her routine, Olivia found herself climbing the two short stairs to the mini-stage. She only performed now when she wanted to, long past the time where she danced for money.

Now she did it for pleasure.

Although there was a pole built into the stage, she ignored it and pulled a chair from behind the stage curtain. She turned it around and sat in it primly, holding up an imaginary mirror and pretending to fix her hair.

All the eyes in the room followed her movements and when the music changed to an even slower tempo, she swayed like she was dancing alone in her room at home.

She uncrossed her legs and then stretched down to caress her legs, stopping to unhook the ankle straps of her shoes. After pulling them off, she kicked them to the side of the stage and stood, swiveling her hips sensually to the music.

Her robe slid down her arm and she allowed it, looking over her now bare shoulder.

King sat forward in his chair, like he was on the verge of charging onstage to get to her.

Emboldened, Olivia shimmied, swinging her hair back and forth sensually, really getting into it now. This was freedom, dancing however she wanted and not caring what anyone thought of her. Up here, she wasn't worried about the club's future, whether Bennett might find out what she did for a living or her broken relationship with her parents.

Right here, right now, she was freedom incarnate.

When the music ended, she turned and winked over her shoulder. Then she kicked the chair out of the way and strode off stage, head held high.

———

She was magnificent.

King watched her sensual dance, just as enraptured as everyone else in the room. It wasn't just that she was beautiful, the word too tepid to describe something as vibrant as his angel.

Angel. He snorted. There was no way that was her real name but it was strangely perfect for her.

She had an unearthly sensuality, every one of her slow movements making him think of naked skin and sweat. She was a walking, talking embodiment of temptation. She was perfect.

By the time she walked off stage, kicking the chair out of the way as she went, every man in the room practically had his tongue hanging out.

Next to him, James clapped and pumped his fist in the air. "Yeah, that's what I'm talking about." He glanced over at King. "You might have met your match with that one, man. She doesn't look like she takes any shit."

King blinked, feeling like he was surfacing after being underwater for hours. Damn it, she'd already gotten under his skin making him wonder if she could take all of him at once or if he'd have to spend more time getting her little pussy ready for him. Whether she'd only be interested in his money or if she'd be that mythical creature he'd always assumed wasn't real, a woman who could see him as just a man.

Would she argue with him in bed too or would she let him take control?

He wasn't sure what kind of magic spell she'd weaved but he shook his head to clear the thought of tangled sheets and warm flesh. It was time to man up. Getting tied in knots over some woman was the last thing he needed. He had to focus.

She *wasn't* perfect. She was perfect to scandalize his parents.

Huge difference.

And as unearthly as she seemed, she was still a woman. Which meant she was motivated by greed, vanity and power, just like everyone else.

All he needed was a chance to get her alone. He would make her an offer and hopefully they would both get what they wanted out of their time together. If they happened to have fantastic sex at the same time, well, he'd consider that a perk of the job.

For the rest of the evening, King kept an eye on the stage curtain and the door she'd originally entered through. There were two other girls working the room and they kept the other guys more than happy, performing a tandem stage routine and then ending the night by giving the groom-to-be a joint lap dance that was unlike anything King had ever seen.

He had to admit, Club VIP had surpassed his expectations in every way. And since the Masquerade room insisted on anonymity with everyone wearing masks, he was less concerned about any pictures that might leak and find their way to the internet.

It was a little after midnight when he saw his opportunity. Devin was passed out on the stage with a feather boa wrapped around his head. Several of the guys had already gone home and the ones that hadn't would be soon. The door in the back of the room opened and his angel stuck her head in, surveying the scene. Trying not to look too interested, King motioned to James, who was bouncing one of the dancers on his lap.

"Can you ride in the limo and make sure everyone gets home?"

James nodded absently. "Sure thing. I'll consider it overtime."

King rolled his eyes. "Whatever. I need to go get my future wife."

In his inebriated state, James found that hilarious. The dancer on his lap giggled and her full breasts swayed, slapping James in the face.

King stood and stepped over the legs, arms and bodies on the floor. He'd stopped drinking hours ago, knowing he'd need all of his wits for this conversation. His angel looked up when he approached and something like fear appeared in her eyes. It was quickly banked behind a sharp, no-nonsense expression.

Interesting, King thought.

"Was the party to your liking, Mr. Kingsley?"

"It was perfect. Devin is happy and so is the rest of my executive staff. Although it means I won't be getting anything productive out of them for the next twenty-four hours, at least."

Her adorable little nose wrinkled. "But it's the weekend?"

Nothing could have illustrated the differences between them so clearly. King couldn't remember the last time the weekend had represented relaxation time. Probably not since he was in grade school. Even in high school he'd been helping his father and learning the business.

"Indeed." He lowered his voice slightly. "This might seem a little strange but I wondered if I could speak with you after the party. I could drive you home."

The wariness re-entered her eyes. "Did you want to discuss the event? We pride ourselves on making sure our members have the fantasy experience of their dreams."

He chuckled. "I don't think any dream I've ever had could even compare. But no, it's not about the event. It's... a private matter."

She nodded. "I see. Why don't you meet me at Shiney's, the pub down the street, in a half hour?"

It hit him then that she didn't want to be alone with him. He kicked himself for not thinking of it but tried to lighten the situation with a little humor.

"Afraid to be alone with me, angel?"

The relief on her face proved she'd been worried about how he'd react. She grinned up at him saucily.

"Not afraid. Cautious. Perhaps you're the one who should be afraid."

Unable to resist, he leaned a little closer, taking in the fresh, lilac scent of her. Of course, it went straight to his dick. He let out a breath and was grateful that they'd come directly from the office. His suit jacket was long enough to hide the huge bulge in his trousers.

"Why is that? You don't look scary to me."

His eyes roamed over her scantily clad form and he suppressed a groan when she turned, angling her round bottom in his direction.

"Looks can be deceiving, Mr. Kingsley."

"King," he interrupted. "Although I've been told it's my fate, I'm not ready to turn into my father just yet."

She winked. "Whatever you say, Your Majesty. Just don't be late."

Chapter 4

Olivia leaned against the bar in Shiney's Pub. It was crowded, which wasn't unusual for the wee hours of a Saturday morning.

Dupont Circle was known to be one of the hubs of D.C. nightlife and tonight was no exception. Girls in short dresses and guys in jeans and tight muscle shirts milled on the dance floor and around the pool table on the other side of the room. Shiney's was known for loud music, dim lighting and strong drinks.

The perfect place to meet a date when you weren't sure if they were a psycho yet.

What the hell are you doing?

Olivia raised her eyebrows at the bartender and he nodded,

indicating that he'd bring her another cranberry juice. It wasn't her favorite after work beverage but she was already walking on the wild side tonight.

If she was going to do something as foolish as meet a strange man after work, she definitely wasn't going to do it with alcohol in her system.

But what a man.

She squirmed remembering how intense he'd been leaning over her, blue eyes fixed on her ass. It had been a really long time since she'd experienced pure, high-octane desire.

This was no civilized thing.

She didn't want him to take her out for dinner and a movie with a polite kiss at the end. Oh no. She wanted his big hands on her breasts, his tongue in her mouth and to find out if that bulge in his pants was as big as it appeared.

He made her want *sex*, pure and simple. Sweaty, rough, dirty sex. Sex that made her feel naughty and liberated all at the same time.

It had been so long since she'd wanted a man. Truthfully, that was probably the only reason she'd said yes. It would probably be a shock to others since she dealt in fantasy but her own desires had been curiously dormant for years.

Maybe it was because she was surrounded by eroticism at the club and she'd become immune to it. Nothing really pushed her buttons any more.

She was bored.

"A whisky. Neat." An arm, lightly covered in dark hair, landed on the bar right next to her. King raised an eyebrow at her drink. "Please tell me there's vodka in that?"

She raised her glass, eyeing him over the brim. "Hoping to get me drunk?"

"Of course. What kind of pervert would I be if I wasn't trying to get you drunk?"

Olivia shook her head, charmed in spite of herself. She snuck a glance at him, taking in the custom tailored suit and the watch that she identified as an Audemars Piguet. Expensive but classy.

He was definitely their typical member. Wealthy, entitled and demanding. However, she hadn't been expecting him to have a sense of humor.

"So are you going to tell me about this personal matter now or do you want to ask for a background check first? Maybe take me to an underground bunker and interrogate me?"

He accepted his drink from the bartender and took a long sip. "I get the sense you think those are overkill? But once you find out about the job, you'll probably prefer the bunker."

Intrigued, Olivia leaned toward him so she could hear better. "You want to offer me a job?"

Then her common sense kicked in and she understood exactly what type of job a guy like *him* would offer to a girl like *her*.

She pushed her drink away and pulled a twenty dollar bill out of her pocket, more than enough to cover her drinks and the tip.

"Wait, you're leaving?" King put his hand on her arm but pulled it back when she glared at him.

"Yes. I'm going home. Despite what you probably think after meeting me at the club, I don't fuck for money. I'm not interested in your *job offer*." She made exaggerated quotation marks with her fingers.

His eyebrows shot up. "Whoa! That's not what I was getting at. I swear. This is a legit job offer. Nothing... inappropriate."

Olivia sat back down, feeling a little foolish. With her luck he'd turn out to be a potential investor in the club or something else completely legitimate and she'd feel even worse.

What was it about this guy? He tied her in knots and made her feel like a teenage girl with her first crush. It was mortifying.

"I'm sorry if I overreacted."

"No apology is necessary. I should have realized how it would sound."

Olivia laughed and then propped her head on her hand. "Regretting this yet? In case you can't tell, I don't get out much."

King smiled. "Not at all. You're perfect. A woman who isn't afraid to state her mind."

There was something in the way he said it that wasn't exactly a compliment but Olivia was too tired to look for hidden meaning. This entire thing was likely a mistake. Her libido had always gotten her into trouble, that was how she'd ended up a pregnant, single college dropout before she was even twenty years old.

She sat up straight and fixed a polite smile on her face. Whatever King wanted, she'd find a way to shut him down politely and then go on with her life. He was a VIP member so she couldn't afford to alienate him but it was high time she stopped letting her panties lead her around.

Men had always been the root of all her troubles but Bennett was going to save her from all that. It was time to stop playing games and go for the right kind of man. Ben was her best friend and she already loved him.

The rest would come with time, right?

King couldn't stop staring at her mouth.

He took another swig of whisky, relishing the smooth burn as it traveled down and settled in the pit of his stomach.

She sat up slightly and smiled at him, a wooden smile that didn't reach her eyes. He'd seen that particular look plenty of times on his mother's face when his father was droning on about something or other.

"You've already decided you're going to say no."

Surprise flickered in her eyes before she glanced away. Her fingers wrapped around her glass but there was nothing left but ice.

"Look... King. I don't want to be rude but I have a feeling whatever you're going to ask me probably isn't something I want to do."

"Oh really? You don't like parties? Or eating exquisite cuisine? Or shopping for clothes and shoes that you don't have to pay for? The job comes with a clothing allowance."

She dipped her head. "Go on. Not that I'm interested or anything."

King pressed his lips together to stifle a grin. "My parents have decided that I need to settle down. I'm the CEO of the family business and as a result, I haven't had much time to meet anyone."

"They're probably just worried about you," she said.

He grimaced. "That may be the case. But they've also decided that they'll hand control over to my little brother if I don't settle down. My little brother who at this very moment is probably out drinking, sleeping with anything on two legs and generally being as much of a spoiled brat as possible."

Angel didn't say anything but he could tell she was listening because she'd angled her head closer to him. It was impossible not to notice how long her eyelashes were or how the tips of her long, wavy hair brushed her lower back. She'd changed into street clothes but he could still see her sweet curves even beneath jeans and a leather jacket.

"So, you need me to pretend to be your girlfriend? Come on. That only works in the movies. You don't think your parents will find it suspicious that you suddenly have a girlfriend? They're going to know you're just pretending to placate them."

"I know."

Her mouth puckered into the most adorable little pout. Damn he was going to enjoy this. His parents would be appropriately scared off by her smart mouth and would leave him, and his position at Kingsley International, alone. Meanwhile, he was going to enjoy having that smart mouth all over him. He'd never been so happy about his parents meddling before.

"Okay, maybe I'm just tired or perhaps there actually was vodka in the cranberry juice but I don't get the point of this. Why bother having me pretend to be your girlfriend if your parents are going to know what you're doing?"

He couldn't resist anymore so he tapped her softly on the end of the nose. She gasped softly and a faint flush covered her cheekbones.

"Because, my sweet angel, my parents know me well. They aren't expecting me to fall in love. They just want me to marry for appearances sake. My parents aren't in love either. My mother's family had some corporate holdings that my father's family was interested in. So they married and now Kingsley International is one of the biggest banking and investing firms in the world."

"That sounds very cold."

"They seem happy enough. But apparently not so happy that they keep their nose out of my business. So here's the deal. I have a meeting next month with some important European investors. I've spent years preparing for this deal. There is no way I can let them pull me off now and stick Colin in there." He winced at just the thought.

"Who's Colin?" Her question brought him back to the matter at hand.

"My little brother. I love him but he'd fuck it up and then I'd have to spend another five years cleaning up the mess by the time my father comes to his senses. I have worked so hard for this. Everyone thinks I got my position just by virtue of my last name but my father made me prove myself every step of the way. I've been at his knee since I was a child learning the ins and outs of our business. While everyone else was partying, I was studying finance and economics, preparing for when I'd finally be old enough to take over. This job is all I have."

He stopped talking to find her watching him, stunned. Embarrassed by how much he'd just revealed, he cleared his throat.

"The point is, I don't have time for this. So let's just play the game for a few weeks and keep my parents happy. You'll get to shop, eat and basically do whatever the hell you want on my dime the entire time. It's a pretty decent deal."

She made a face. "Are you really going to pretend you don't have a long list of girls who'd be more than happy to wine and dine on your tab?"

Uncomfortable, he took another swig of his drink. How could he explain things without sounding like even more of an entitled jerk than what she already thought?

"I've had girlfriends, sure. But this is just a short-term thing."

She snorted. "Of course. Wouldn't want any of them getting the wrong idea. They might actually think you *gasp* liked them! How inconvenient."

"Did you just say gasp? As in, actually say the word out loud?"

"Did you just say you can't ask any of the girls you already know because it would be hard to get rid of them afterward?" She pantomimed putting her fingers down her throat.

Oh yeah, his father was going to shit a brick when he brought her home.

"I didn't actually say that but if we're being blunt, then yes. Giving someone false hope doesn't seem like the kindest thing to do."

She shrugged. "Well, I guess that's true. But it doesn't mean I'm participating in this nonsense either. Good luck!" She stood and straightened her jacket.

"I'll pay you ten grand for the month," he blurted out.

Her mouth fell open. "How much?"

Normally an expert negotiator, King couldn't believe he'd just thrown a number out there with no forethought. She was already going to hose him in clothing and spa charges so he hadn't been planning to offer any kind of salary.

After all, what woman wouldn't jump at the chance to buy all the clothes, shoes and whatever other shit women bought on someone else's credit card?

"You heard me. Are you in or what?"

It came out more aggressively than he'd intended but he was still grouchy about being put in a corner.

The bartender leaned over, interrupting their tense stand-off. "You ready to close out, Livvy?"

She pulled her eyes away from his and handed over some cash. "Yeah, I'm done Jeb. Keep the change."

"You got it."

The bartender glanced over at him so King pulled out his wallet and handed over the first credit card his fingers touched.

"Charge her drinks to my tab. Keep the cash for yourself."

The bartender didn't look impressed at his largesse but took the card.

She crossed her arms. "Okay."

"Okay," he echoed. "You'll do it?"

She nodded and pulled out a small business card from the inner pocket of her jacket. "Here's my card, my cell number is on the back. Let me know when you need me. Don't worry about the clothes. I've got that covered."

She turned and he reached out before he thought, panicked at the thought of her leaving without him. He wanted to walk her to her car and make sure she was safe, a completely alien feeling, but the bartender still had his card so instead he stood there patting her arm like an idiot.

"He called you Livvy."

Her lips curled up. "You didn't really think my name was Angel, did you?" She stuck out her hand. "Olivia."

He shook it. "Olivia. I'll call you tomorrow, Olivia."

She winked. "I'll answer."

People moved out of the way as she walked though the crowd, as if they too could sense the power in the swing of her hips. There was something hypnotic about the way she moved. It made him think he could enjoy watching her do anything and not just the dirty things he'd been unable to stop imagining the entire time they were talking.

He'd love to watch her dance when she thought no one was watching, or sing in the shower or wiggle that perky little behind while she brushed her teeth in the morning. The door to the pub swung shut behind her and King groaned.

"You don't look so good." The bartender held out his card, watching him with a knowing smile on his face.

"I'm not. I'm completely fucked."

Chapter 5

Olivia woke the next morning with a pounding head and vaguely nauseous, despite not having any alcohol the prior night. She groaned and pulled the covers over her head. That was how King affected her. He made her feel like she'd been flattened by a truck.

He definitely knew how to get her interest.

Whose parents required them to get married by a certain age anymore? There was something weird about the whole thing. It sounded like some sort of medieval plot.

But the rich were different. She knew that better than most after growing up on the periphery of their world. They had totally different morals and ethics. For all she knew, he might be lying about the whole thing to get closer to her.

She knew all about what rich men wanted from girls like her.

Then she remembered the look in his eye. He'd spoken about this business deal with real passion. He really wanted it. To a man like King, business was everything. She shouldn't care that this was obviously so important to him.

You don't even know him.

But that was the thing. She felt like she did. Or at least, she knew that feeling of wanting to be more. Wanting to have more.

Well, either way it was an insane amount of money. She could put up with him for ten grand. Especially if all she had to do was show up and pretend she didn't hate him at a bunch of events.

What the hell am I going to wear?

She reached over to her phone on the nightstand. Elle would definitely have something appropriate and wouldn't mind if she borrowed a few things. Although knowing her friend she wasn't going to get off without a full explanation about why she needed fancy clothes all of a sudden. It was still better than having King buy her clothes. There weren't going to be any *Pretty Woman* moments between them. No, thanks.

Her heart screeched to a halt when she saw a text from an unfamiliar number.

- Dinner party at my parents' house tonight. I'll pick you up at seven. Text me your address. - K

Olivia swallowed, her throat suddenly as dry as the Sahara. She hadn't been expecting him to need her so quickly.

Shit.

As her fingers flew over the keys composing a text to Elle, she could only hope her friend wasn't out of town or she would have to charge a dress to her credit card. Just the thought burned. It had taken her so long to work her way out of debt that she hated to charge anything now.

Luckily, it didn't take long for Elle to respond. Just as she thought, Elle not only didn't mind her borrowing a few things but she had extra clothes in her office at the club. That was perfect. She had a good excuse to meet King there instead of her house. There was no way she wanted that smooth talker anywhere near her bedroom.

As expected, after her initial texts telling her where to find the clothes, Elle quickly narrowed in on the real issue.

- And why do we need fancy clothes?

- There's this guy... Not sure where it's going but I don't want to look like a complete hick in front of his parents.

- You're meeting the parents? Where have I been? I didn't even know you were seeing anyone.

- It's a new thing but we're going to be at a party his parents are hosting so. Anyway, wish me luck!

She could only hope that Elle was still too tired to question her strange response. Olivia wasn't entirely sure of her own motivation at this point and she definitely couldn't explain it to anyone else.

She could go with the obvious explanation and blame it on the money. How many people could turn down ten thousand dollars? It would give her some much needed breathing room and ensure that she had a cushion for any unexpected expenses.

All it would take was one health issue and she'd be back in debt. Someone like King had no idea how close the average person was to bankruptcy at any time. Most were only one car accident away from losing everything they owned.

Olivia flopped back on the bed and covered her face with her arm. The amount of energy she was wasting on this guy was ridiculous. She should just tell him she'd changed her mind and then she wouldn't have to stress about this. But ten thousand dollars...

She didn't want her partners to ever know just how thin she'd stretched herself to afford her share of the club. It was worth it though, no question.

To have the freedom to be her own boss, she'd eat ramen noodles and cut coupons and give up every luxury. That had been her life for the past few years and she was finally almost comfortable.

That ten thousand dollars would be an extra cushion in her *I'll never have to ask my parents for money again* fund. Her pride was worth any amount of discomfort she felt in King's presence.

So he was sexy, so what? She'd dealt with sexy, entitled alpha A-holes before. He was no different. She would do the job, impress his parents and never look back.

She sat up and grabbed her phone again. After texting King to meet her at the club, she threw back the comforter and stretched. First thing she wanted to do was get in a workout.

If her completely neglected body could work up this much enthusiasm for a guy she wasn't even sure she liked, then it could handle a little cardio. She would work off her newfound sexual appetite in the gym.

———

*L*ater that evening, King checked his watch for the hundredth time. Why the hell was he so nervous?

He was picking up a stripper with the intention of horrifying his parents. But the entire day when he should have been reviewing the financials of a company Kingsley International was interested in acquiring, he was thinking about her pert little mouth instead.

He parked outside the club and his eyes immediately traveled to the small figure walking his way. She must have been watching him from inside. It was a chilly day with a brisk wind so he appreciated the courtesy. He wouldn't have to get out of the warm car.

She opened the passenger side door and climbed inside, bringing the scent of lavender with her.

"Good evening. I hope you weren't waiting long."

She shook her head. "No, I've only been here about ten minutes. There was some stuff I needed in the office, that's why I wanted to meet here."

He was pretty sure she just didn't want him having her address but he didn't mention it. It would probably freak her out to know that he already knew her address, what kind of car she drove and how much money was currently in her bank account at First National Bank and Trust.

There wasn't too much he couldn't find out if he paid enough.

"There aren't going to be any ex-girlfriends at this party, right? I'm willing to help you out but I draw the line at fighting some jealous chick. I won't even fight for a guy I'm actually dating."

He chuckled. "No jealous ex-girlfriends you need to worry about. Just a bunch of people drinking too much and trying to impress my father. A typical weekend at the Kingsley stronghold."

"Sounds fun."

Her voice was so droll that it only made him smile harder. Somehow, talking about it with her, made it easier to contemplate spending the next few hours under his parents' roof. He could already see her making that annoyed face at some older guy who dared to look at her the wrong way.

She turned in her seat and regarded him with curious eyes. "So, what's the deal?"

He must have looked as confused as he felt because she rolled her eyes. It was a struggle to keep his eyes on the road when all her wiggling in the seat had worked her dress up her legs several inches.

"Don't give me that look. You know what I mean. Am I supposed to be someone you've dated forever and we're supposed to pretend like we're madly in love? I'm not good at subterfuge."

"No, just be yourself. If anyone asks you a question, you're to answer it completely honestly."

He was looking forward to this dinner party with a level of enthusiasm that he'd never thought to attach to one of his parents' events.

Normally he didn't go for the ballbuster type but there was something incredibly arousing about Olivia's smart mouth. She hadn't hesitated to call him on his shit yet and he had no doubt that she wouldn't hold back tonight.

How many times had he fantasized about telling one of his father's stuffed shirt friends what he really thought about them?

He grinned. He'd have to stick close to her tonight. The first time one of those good-old-boys said the wrong thing to Olivia, it was going to be like watching a cage match live and in person.

"Seriously? You want me to be completely honest?"

"Yes. Keeping track of lies is too complicated and that's how people get caught. We met yesterday. I asked you out. That's as much truth as anyone needs."

"I doubt anyone there is ready for my brand of truth," she mumbled.

King didn't think they were either. His father was probably going to beg him not to get married after tonight.

"So we're just going with the truth. Okay." She looked out the window and clenched and unclenched her first.

As if suddenly aware of her fidgeting, she forced her hand open and pressed it against her thigh.

She's nervous.

The thought didn't make him feel any better. He couldn't help feeling a little guilty. He was basically throwing her to the wolves in a way.

He could only imagine how his parents were going to react when she told them King had picked her up in a pleasure club after watching one of his employees get a lap dance.

But his parents and sister were too concerned about appearances to actually say anything. They would more than likely just grit their teeth and then give him an earful later.

He squelched the unusual feelings of guilt and focused on the road. If tonight went as planned, he'd horrify his parents so badly they'd abandon this ridiculous idea of marrying him off and let him get back to what he was so good at.

Making money.

Chapter 6

For the rest of the drive, they rode in silence. Olivia tried to keep from fidgeting but all the excess energy in her body had to go somewhere.

She'd thought that working out earlier in the day would make her calm, in control. However, all it had done was amp her up even more. She'd been on edge all evening, almost poking her eye out with the wand while putting on her mascara.

For a woman who was used to performing, she was in uneasy territory. She wasn't used to trying to blend in. Her living revolved around being the center of attention, making sure that when she was in a room, all eyes were on her.

But that wasn't why she was here. Tonight, she wasn't the star of the show but a supporting player. The whole goal this evening was to help King smooth things over with his parents.

She still wasn't sure she understood their dynamic. He seemed completely unconcerned with whether they even liked her and seemed convinced that they'd be happy with just the appearance of him being coupled up. But men could be a little dense about these things so she suspected the truth was a little more nuanced than that.

What parents didn't want their child to be happy?

He might think they didn't care about the girl he brought home but she was willing to bet they would want to see some kind of affection between them.

She glanced over at him. Even in profile he looked harsh, like a monarch surveying the peasants he ruled over. Although from where he was sitting that probably wasn't too far from the truth.

The car glided to a stop and King stepped out. She'd been so deep in thought that she hadn't paid the slightest attention to where they were. King had told her his parents lived in Arlington, a wealthy suburb in the neighboring state of Virginia.

Olivia sat up, looking around with interest. They were parked on a circular drive in front of a massive house.

House was probably not even the right term. It was a red brick structure with two long wings on the sides that wrapped around enclosing them in a courtyard. The front door was flanked by twin white columns that made her think of *Gone with The Wind.* All the windows on both stories were lit up.

She whistled softly right before King opened her door. "Are we at a hotel?" she joked.

His lips twitched. "This is my parents' estate. Kingsley Manor."

She accepted his hand and didn't resist when he pulled her arm through his. It was a little late for second thoughts but she had to admit it was easier to go forward with him so close.

Even though he drove her slightly crazy and his arrogance annoyed her, she'd always felt safe with him. Something she would have to examine at a later date.

The front doors opened and King greeted the uniformed man with a warm smile.

"Hello, Jenner. How are things this evening?"

The older man took their coats and waved them in with a flourish of his hand. "Busy, sir. You know your mother. She's never idle."

King grunted and Olivia realized he was staring at her dress, revealed when she'd removed her coat. It wasn't anything extraordinary just your standard little black dress but it had a sweetheart neckline that framed her bust perfectly.

Self-conscious, she tugged at the fabric as discreetly as she could. The dress fit technically, even though she was way taller than Elle.

She bit her lip.

Okay, Elle was not only shorter but a lot bigger in the bust too. The loose fit showed a little more cleavage than she liked but she hadn't thought it was *that* noticeable.

"What? Is the dress too short?" she finally asked, when she couldn't take his staring anymore.

He shook his head, the angry look on his face dissolving into his usual placid expression. "Nothing. You are stunning."

"I... thank you."

It was such a strange compliment. The words were kind but he looked almost pissed off about it. Like he was annoyed to be attracted to her.

She wasn't sure what to think of that. There shouldn't be any surprises. Maybe the dress was a tad too short but he'd seen what she looked like before at the club in *way* more detail. He was lucky she hadn't worn something with a split up her leg and half of her cleavage coming out.

Before she could think on it too long, a woman with platinum blond hair approached.

"King? There you are darling. I was wondering if you weren't coming."

King kissed her on both cheeks just as a distinguished older man appeared at his elbow. He looked a lot like King so she assumed this was his father.

"Olivia, this is my mother, Fiona Kingsley. Mother, this is Olivia-" King stopped abruptly and then laughed. "I'm sorry, I actually don't know your last name."

An awkward silence fell over the group and Liv could feel a blush creeping over her cheeks. Geez, maybe instead of stressing out on the way there they should have been exchanging the basic information.

"It's Reyes. Olivia Reyes." She extended her hand and a beat before she would have withdrawn it, his mother took it.

"Lovely to meet you, Olivia. This is King's father, Thane the Third."

"Oh, you're named for your father. That's nice."

King rolled his eyes but she guessed his father must have agreed because he accepted her hand looking slightly more pleasant.

"Yes it is, isn't it? It's an honor to carry a name that goes back for generations."

Fiona patted her husband's chest distractedly. "Of course it is, dear. Now Olivia, how did you and King meet?"

The blush that had started to recede marginally came back full force.

"Oh, we met yesterday."

She glanced over at King who was watching everything with a strange little smile. He didn't seem inclined to jump in and make this less awkward so she grabbed his arm and squeezed.

"Actually would you excuse us for a moment?" She walked back toward the hallway, dragging him behind her.

———

King allowed Olivia to drag him along until they reached the living room. All of the furniture had been moved out to make room for a dance floor. After a split second of thought, he tugged on Olivia's hand until she turned and tumbled into his arms.

He guided her until they were moving smoothly with the other couples. The band for the event consisted of a harpist, a violinist and a flute player. King sighed. If his blood wasn't rushing from being plastered against Olivia's shapely body, he'd be on the verge of falling asleep already.

She glared up at him. "What the hell was that back there?"

He looked around. Her sharp words hadn't gone unnoticed. The couple dancing right next to them looked at them in shock and then moved a little further away.

Good.

Maybe she'd cuss him out right here and now and they could get this over with.

"What do you mean? My parents seemed to like you."

She pulled back putting some space between them. Her eyes narrowed but she didn't say anything else.

"King! I can't believe you're actually here!"

Olivia jumped back as he was tackled from the side. He managed to keep from falling on his ass as his sister, Georgina, threw her arms around his neck.

Olivia watched with amusement. *Ex-girlfriend*, she mouthed.

He could see why she might think that. His sister was gorgeous and he didn't just think that because she looked a little like him with her long dark hair and sky blue eyes. He'd had to come to terms with it after fending off quite a few of his friends who'd shown interest.

"Georgie, this is Olivia. The girl you just shoved out of the way just now. Olivia, this is my little sister, Georgina."

Georgie turned and clapped her hands over her mouth. "Oh my god, I'm so sorry!"

Olivia glanced between them and then her eyes bugged out as Georgie enveloped her in an enthusiastic hug.

"I get a little excited sometimes. My brother always says I'm like a terrier when I get worked up."

Olivia glanced at him. "That's okay. Not everyone can be a robot like King."

Georgie giggled. "Exactly! That's what I always say too. You should come meet my friends!"

This evening was quickly getting out of control. King needed Olivia with him so they could do something inappropriate and get his father to back off his maddening plan to force him to settle down. They couldn't do that if she was off talking about nail polish or whatever inane nonsense his little sister and her friends talked about.

"Wait a minute, you're stealing my date?"

Georgie rolled her eyes. "It's not like we're going that far. You can survive without her for a few minutes."

Before he could say anything else, Georgie had Olivia by the arm. He stood there awkwardly, watching as they were stopped by his father. Olivia said something he couldn't hear and his father's laughter rang out through the room.

He hadn't heard his father laugh like that in a long time.

"Damn it." King stalked over to the bar. He'd just ordered a scotch when his father appeared at his elbow.

"Glad to see you're taking this seriously, son. She's a beautiful girl. Not what I expected but somehow she seems to have your number."

He glanced over his shoulder to where Olivia held court in the middle of Georgie's friends. She was telling some story, her hands moving around her face animatedly and the entire group erupted in laughter. The women seemed to have accepted her as one of their own already and he'd noticed more than a few men eyeing her.

He gritted his teeth. This evening was definitely not going according to plan so far.

The only way his father would back off was if he saw for himself what a liability the wrong wife could be. But Olivia wasn't doing any of the things he'd expected. He'd expected her to come inappropriately dressed and scandalize them.

Instead she was charming the women and inspiring lust and envy in the men.

"So, I've been doing some more research on AliCorp and they're prime for a merger. Our meeting next week should be nothing more than a formality at this point."

His father nodded. "I'm not worried about it. You've never let me down."

Instead of making him feel better, the words enraged him, mainly because of how true they were. He'd dedicated his entire life to making his father proud and working to ensure that the Kingsley name represented excellence.

"I've never let you down and yet you've threatened to turn it all over to Colin if I don't do what you want?"

His father clapped him on the back. "Your brother isn't as daft as you think he is. He just needs someone to believe in him. You, on the other hand, need to learn an entirely different lesson."

"Please. Enlighten me, Dad. Because I don't get it at all."

His father regarded him for a long moment. Then suddenly his brown eyes looked weary. "I know you don't. All I can hope is that you'll figure it out before it's too late."

____

Chapter 7

____

*K*ing groaned and swallowed the last of his scotch. Another round of laughter came from the corner of the room. That was it. He put his glass down on the bar and pushed his way through the crowd. The laughter petered off as he shouldered his way through. Olivia peered up at him with innocent eyes.

"Hi, King. Is everything okay?"

She didn't say anything else but he got the definite impression that she was laughing at him.

"No, everything is not okay. I haven't gotten to see you all night."

In hindsight, that wasn't at all what he'd meant to say. He'd wanted to remind her that she was supposed to be helping him and not socializing but somehow it came out sounding more like the complaint of a jealous lover.

Like he... missed her. Which was ridiculous, of course.

He scowled when the girls all sighed and cooed about how romantic it was. His own damn sister was no help. She put her arm around Olivia and squeezed.

"I've never seen my brother like this, Livvy. He's always a grump but he usually doesn't care about anything except business."

King gritted his teeth so hard it felt like his jaw would lock in that position. Olivia must have sensed he was nearing the end of his patience because she carefully extricated herself from the group and took his hand.

"Well, ladies, it's been fun. But I think I'd better dance with my man before some other girl throws herself in his arms." She winked at his sister. "See you later, Georgie."

He didn't wait around to see what his sister would reply. With the way the night was going she'd come up with some other reason to keep Olivia away from him. Bypassing the dance floor, he made his way through the kitchen to the back stairs. Olivia rushed to keep up with him, the sound of her high heels on the polished wood floors like gunshots.

"Where are we going in such a hurry? And why are we leaving the party? I thought the whole idea was to mingle."

She huffed out an exasperated breath as he led her up the stairs and down a hallway. Then he pulled her through the second door on the left. As soon as she cleared the threshold, he closed the door and pushed her against it.

"King, what–"

Whatever she'd been about to say was swallowed as he attacked her mouth. His hands were all over the place, under her dress and in her hair, trying to take in every inch of her at once.

She melted against him and wrapped her hands around him, shoving his suit jacket to the side so she could get closer. Their tongues tangled as he tried to get more of her taste. Her lavender and lilac scent was all over him and he abandoned her mouth to kiss his way down her throat, trying to find the source of the drugging scent.

He lifted her under the thighs, hefting her higher so he could settle between her thighs. When his cock, rigid in the confines of his suit pants, nestled against what he knew had to be itty bitty panties, she let out a throaty moan.

Any remaining blood in his brain quickly abandoned ship and flowed south.

He'd never been this hard, this needy, this desperate before. He could give a shit about his parents downstairs or what they thought of him right now. His entire world condensed to right here, right now, and whether or not Liv was going to let him inside her soft, wet heat.

"King, what the hell are we doing?" she gasped. Her lips attached to his neck and placed suctioning kisses all the way up to his ear. She took the lobe between her teeth and bit down gently, causing him to cry out.

"Fuck, bite me again."

She moaned and bit him again, this time right below his ear. His last bit of restraint snapped and he fumbled with the front of his pants, almost ripping the zipper off in his haste. Olivia chuckled as he struggled to push his pants down. Her laughter cut off abruptly when he nudged into position, easing through her wet folds until she took him to the root.

"King. *Oh my god.*"

She shuddered and satisfaction stormed through his veins. He'd put that look on her face. He'd drawn every one of those helpless, erotic sounds from her throat. *Him.*

She was all his.

He grabbed her hands in one of his and held them over her head, forcing her to hold still as he established a hard rhythm, angling so she'd get tons of friction right where it counted.

It wasn't long before her moans turned into soft whimpers. King struggled to hold it together as she exploded beneath him, her legs tightening around his back as she rode out her release.

He pressed his face against her neck, panting with the effort it took to hold back, trying to prolong her pleasure. Then she clamped down on him and his mind went blank. He lost it as his own orgasm swamped him and his legs went so weak he almost dropped her.

He managed to hold it together and keep them upright. By the time he came back to himself, she was breathing deeply and he felt like every one of his muscles had been wrung out.

A small bit of his reason returned and he acknowledged that taking her in his childhood bedroom while his parents and their friends were right downstairs wasn't the best course of action. But even more than that, was the fact that after such a small taste of her, he only wanted more. The enormity of how much he wanted her frightened him.

He was supposed to be getting her out of his system, not sinking in deeper and deeper.

"We should get back."

He pulled out gently and set her on her feet. She stood up straight and then she paled slightly.

"Oh no. We didn't use anything."

King reared back in shock. He closed his eyes. How could he have been so careless?

He'd never forgotten a condom before, not even when he was drunk. It wasn't the kind of thing a man in his position could afford to be careless about.

She held up a hand before he could speak. "It's okay, I'm on the pill."

"Even so, you have every right to be angry. I can't believe I forgot. I'm so sorry, Olivia."

She straightened her dress and pulled the bra back into place. "It was an accident. How can I be angry when I didn't remember either? You make me forget everything."

They both arranged their clothes and tried not to look at each other.

God, this was awkward.

Olivia touched his arm. "King, about what happened. Just... don't pay me. This was... just don't pay me anything, okay?" She blushed deeply and then tugged at the top of her dress. "Maybe we should go back now."

Her words brought a whole new element to his discomfort. He'd forgotten all about their deal. Everything that had happened tonight was completely off-script. The only thing he'd been thinking about tonight was Olivia and how she affected him.

"Yeah. We should go." King reached behind her and opened the door.

She walked out without looking back.

What the hell was he really doing here? His plan was clearly a failure since his parents and his sister seemed to like her. Sure, he could tell them the real story of where he'd met her but after watching Olivia in action, he had a feeling they wouldn't care.

The only one in danger here, was him. Every moment he spent in her company would only make it harder to walk away.

It was time to bring this experiment to a close.

Chapter 8

Three weeks later...

Olivia double-checked her appearance in the mirrored elevator doors. When her mother called to make sure she was still coming to their fundraiser, she'd been so tempted to make an excuse.

However, no matter what had ever happened between them, she wouldn't embarrass her parents. Even though that was all they expected from her anyway.

The doors opened and she stepped out into the main lobby of the Ritz-Carlton hotel. Her parents had started *Racing for a Cure* when she was only a child, gathering their peers in the horse ranching industry to support a cure for breast cancer.

Her mother had beaten the disease but had been deter-mined to use her position to advocate for all of the women who didn't have the same resources.

She was so fiercely proud of everything her mother had accomplished in the years since then. Despite her tense relationship with her father, she would put on a smile and charm the attendees into opening their wallets.

This day wasn't about her or how incredibly stupid she was for once again falling for the wrong man.

Just the thought of him made the headache that had been lingering behind her right eye for the past few days throb dangerously. She blew out a breath, determined not to let thoughts of him derail her night.

What had she really expected? For him to call her the next day? To become her boyfriend? To take her out and listen to her and spend all night whispering sweet nothings in her ear?

Gah!

She could just kick herself for allowing even the idea of him into her thoughts. Thane Kingsley *the freaking Fourth,* and yes she'd looked up his full name on his Club VIP paperwork, was an ass. An entitled trust fund baby and a double douchebag of the highest order.

She had clearly gone way too long without a man if he could affect her this strongly after only one night.

But Bennett had really stepped up to fill the void. She smiled thinking of her best friend. Normally so shy, she hadn't expected him to ever initiate their phone conversations or call her just to check on her. But for the past three weeks, he'd been so attentive.

He was still awkward, it was Bennett after all, but he was making such an effort to be there for her. She'd tried to play it cool the first time they'd spoken after her ill-timed night with King but somehow she'd ended up spilling the whole story.

Bennett had listened, asked questions and even offered up some useful advice. He'd asked her to come up early before the award ceremony so they could hang out. It had been years since they'd had time to spend together doing absolutely nothing.

She'd been completely right about Bennett. They were going to be great together.

Once she got all thoughts of the double douchebag out of her head!

Having been to this hotel for prior year's galas, she knew exactly where to go. Her mother stood just inside the doors of the main ballroom wearing a gorgeous bright blue floor-length gown.

Daniela Reyes was still a beautiful woman and for a moment, Olivia was overcome with sadness. Even though she talked to her mother on the phone every week, their once close relationship had grown distant.

When she'd gotten pregnant, her father had been livid and wouldn't allow her in the house and her mother hadn't stood up to him. With time and distance, Olivia didn't really blame her mother. She was a soft-spoken woman, easily flustered by harsh words and confrontation. Though she'd come around to forgiveness, their relationship had never been the same.

"Olivia! You look so beautiful, baby."

"Thanks, Mom. Where's Daddy?"

Her mother looked across the ballroom. Olivia followed her gaze to where her father stood talking to someone she didn't recognize.

"That's Senator Denton. I believe they play golf together."

They watched as her father shook hands with the Senator before walking toward them. Her father acknowledged her presence with a nod. She hated it but his scrutiny immediately made her stand up straighter.

"Good, you're here. I was worried you'd be late."

"She was early, Alberto. Stop worrying. Everything is going exactly as planned. I have a feeling we'll raise even more money this year."

Her father's stern expression softened slightly as her mother adjusted his tie. Daniela was the only person her father ever spared his smiles on. As if he could hear her thoughts, his eyes swung to her. He frowned slightly taking in her bare shoulders.

"Don't you have a wrap? That dress is too revealing, Olivia."

Her shoulders slumped. Her dress was strapless but it was a modest neckline and floor length. She hadn't thought anyone would be scandalized by the sight of her bare shoulders.

"Young people these days don't carry wraps, Alberto. Don't be so old-fashioned," Daniela chuckled.

Her father didn't look convinced but for once he didn't argue his point.

"Just don't offend anyone. This is an important night for your mother. Try not to embarrass us."

"Alberto!" Her mother glared at him until he lowered his gaze. She turned back to Olivia. "He didn't mean that, *mija*."

"It's okay, Mom. I know what he meant. I know I can be blunt sometimes."

Olivia opened her evening clutch and pretending to look for her phone, determined not to let even a single tear fall. What was the point?

She'd always known that her father was ashamed of her. He didn't even know how she made a living. She wasn't sure if he ever checked the balance on her trust fund to know that she hadn't touched a penny of it since her accident.

Even if he knew she wasn't using that money, he probably assumed she was a mistress for a wealthy man. For years, she'd tried to conform, to make herself fit the mold her father wanted and it was not only unsuccessful but painful trying to bend herself into shapes that would never come naturally.

Well, no more.

Nothing she ever did would be good enough for him so from now on she wasn't even going to try. This was the last time she'd bother with keeping up appearances. She was done.

Olivia snagged a glass of champagne from the tray of a passing waiter. She would mingle, smile widely and speak as little as possible. Then as soon as a respectable amount of time passed, she was going home.

There was nothing here for her anymore.

Chapter 9

Fate is playing games with me, King thought. That was the only logical explanation.

For the past three weeks he'd done everything to distance himself from Olivia. He'd given his Club VIP membership key to James. He'd taken her number out of his phone to reduce the chances that he'd give in one night and drunk dial her.

Which had been a real possibility. It was embarrassing to admit because he could usually hold his liquor very well but he'd seen the bottom of more than a few bottles of scotch since then. Hell, he couldn't even visit his family without one of them bringing up her name.

Olivia was so sweet.

Olivia was so funny.

When are you going to bring Olivia around again?

His parents had never been so eager to see *him* and he was their flesh and blood!

How arrogant he'd been to think he could just walk away and not look back. She was never far from his thoughts, no matter what he was doing. He ached for her and it was more than just physical. He wanted to see her eyes light up when she challenged him.

No one ever talked to him like that. He was used to people saying what they thought he wanted to hear.

Olivia hadn't cared about impressing him. She'd just been herself. Which, it turned out, was exactly what he needed.

Now after all of his failed efforts to forget about her, his parents roped him into attending a charity gala with them and here she was. He glanced up at the ceiling briefly.

Message received. I won't fuck it up this time.

It would be a cruel twist of fate if he was pining away and Olivia had gone on with her life like nothing had happened. She might have even met someone else.

The thought made him stop in his tracks. His father looked back in confusion. His mother walked on, greeting someone she knew, oblivious to his distress.

"What's the matter, son? Did you see someone you know?"

He lifted his chin and gestured to the other side of the room. "Do you know the couple that just walked in?"

His father glanced over. "With the wife in the blue dress? Actually, I do. He's the one hosting this event. His wife is a breast cancer survivor." His father laughed suddenly. "Is that Olivia? Well, what do you know. I didn't realize she was related to Alberto Reyes. One of his horses almost took the Preakness last year!"

King didn't follow horse racing at all but even he knew that was huge. His brow furrowed. Why hadn't Olivia told him about her family? Not that he'd given her many opportunities.

He cursed himself again. He'd been so focused on what he needed that he hadn't given her the chance to share much about herself. Everything he knew was gleaned from observation.

She was brash, quick-witted and obviously only working at Club VIP for fun if her family was as wealthy as it appeared.

"Come on, let's go say hello."

"No, wait."

But it was too late. His father was already halfway across the room. He trailed behind, uneasy about how Olivia would respond after the way he'd ghosted on her. He would have preferred to initiate contact in a more private setting.

By the time he caught up, his father was shaking hands with Mr. Reyes and Olivia was watching him approach with a deer-in-headlights look. She apparently hadn't expected to see him again so soon, or ever, either. Then her expression hardened and she whispered something to the woman he assumed was her mother.

He would have expected the silent treatment but as usual, his brash Olivia took the initiative, although she addressed his father instead of him.

"Mr. Kingsley. What a surprise to see you here. It's so nice to see you again."

Mr. Reyes looked between them uneasily. "Olivia, you know Mr. Kingsley?"

His father guffawed. "Your daughter is making an honest man of my oldest boy here. It looks like we'll be seeing a lot more of each other now, Alberto."

Mr. Reyes glanced at him in surprise before extending his hand. "Well, that's nice to hear. Your father is very proud of what you've accomplished at Kingsley International. He brags about you all the time. It's a fine thing to have a son to carry on your work."

Olivia winced slightly but then her smile returned full force. King clenched his fist at his side. This was a side of her he'd never seen. The dutiful daughter holding her tongue and pretending her father's callous words didn't hurt.

It made him want to plow his fist into something.

He'd spent the past three weeks fantasizing about kissing that lush mouth again. Now all he wanted to do was stand in front of her and protect her from the arrows that only family know how to aim so accurately.

"Actually sir, I hope you and your wife don't mind if I borrow Olivia for a dance."

"You kids go on and dance. Don't hang out here with us old folks." Mrs. Reyes beamed at him and nudged Olivia in his direction. She looked like an older version of her daughter with short, curly hair.

King held out his arm and Olivia curled her fingers around his forearm. He led her into the middle of the ballroom so they'd be obscured by the other dancers. For what he was planning, he needed cover. First, he was getting Olivia away from her toxic father and then he would apologize for the way he'd left things.

Then he was getting her out of that dress.

———

If Olivia could have held her nose without looking like a total weirdo, she would have done it. As it was, she tried to hold her breath. It was the only way to ignore how good he smelled.

There hadn't been any way to decline dancing with him without causing a scene but that didn't mean she had to like it.

Except, she definitely liked it.

"I've been thinking about this for weeks. Ever since that night. All I can see when I close my eyes is your face when you came. I haven't gotten any work done."

His voice was rough in her ear as they danced and the deep timbre sent a delicious tingle down her spine.

"Whose fault is that?" she mumbled back, trying so hard not to be affected by that sexy voice growling in her ear.

"Yours. Entirely. You and those sexy lips." His hands tightened on her back and he held her closer.

The position made it obvious that he was just as affected by the conversation as she was. The thick length pressing against her belly was proof of that.

"Apparently you didn't have that hard of a time since I haven't heard from you."

She hated herself for letting him know she'd waited for the call. Her pride wanted him to think she didn't care. Hah! See how he liked that. She should let him think his love-making was so unremarkable she hadn't even missed his presence in her life at all.

Jokes on you, Your Majesty. I have screaming orgasms against random bedroom doors all the time!

Even as she thought it, Olivia knew she could never pull off a nonchalant vibe when it came to how Thane Kingsley IV made love. She was on the verge of having a heart attack just thinking about it. She pulled back slightly, already overheating.

"We need to get out of here," he rasped.

Olivia had never wanted anything more. However, her parents liked having the whole family present throughout the event. Her father seemed to think it was good press for them to be photographed together smiling and happy.

Olivia thought it was ridiculous. By the end of the night, most of the patrons were too drunk and happy themselves to care whether she was there or not.

"My parents will notice if I'm gone. I can't do that to my mom. This is her event. She'll be hurt if I leave without saying goodbye."

"Not if I ask my parents to distract them."

"Why would they do that?"

"Because my father wants me married. If he thinks giving me time alone with you will get me closer to that goal, then he'll do anything I ask him to."

He sent a text to his father. Then grabbed her by the arm.

"Where are we going?"

He glared at her, as if his arousal were all her fault. *And it was*, Olivia thought with satisfaction.

"Somewhere I can take care of *you*." He glanced down at the now noticeable bulge in the front of his pants. "And somewhere I can take care of *this*."

Olivia gulped.

Chapter 10

*K*ing knew there would probably be talk the next day after the way he'd practically dragged Olivia from the ballroom.

He couldn't care any less.

He was done trying to deny the effect she had on him. Clearly she was the one woman he couldn't maintain his cool façade with and if he was going to give in, he'd be damned if he didn't get exactly what he wanted in the process.

Olivia, naked and willing.

The valet pulled his car up and he tipped him generously, after helping Olivia into the passenger seat. Normally he'd have wanted to show off a little, maybe tell her about the completely over the top Maybach Landaulet convertible he'd just had to have.

Instead he bit his lip, trying to hold back all the filthy things he was sure would spill out if he attempted to engage her in conversation. They rode in silence until he turned into the underground garage of his condo building on the North West side of the city.

Olivia sat up in her seat. "Where are we? I thought you were taking me home."

He pulled into one of his parking spaces. The other two were occupied by his Range Rover and the Bentley he liked to drive on occasion.

"I am. My home."

Olivia crossed her arms. "You are so infuriating. Do you ever think about asking what someone else wants?"

"I know what you want, angel. And I'm going to give it to you. Much slower this time and it'll for damn sure last longer."

He got out of the car without waiting for her response which would have probably been to slap him. Not that he wouldn't enjoy a little slap and tickle but he'd rather not put on a show for any neighbors who might be in the garage.

Olivia got out of the car before he could open her door. Surprisingly, she didn't argue with him but followed quietly as he led her to the elevator. Another man rode up with them and she exchanged polite hellos while King remained silent, his eyes on the digital numbers as they rose higher. He didn't care about exchanging pleasantries.

His neighbors already knew he was an asshole.

After the other man got off, it was only about thirty seconds before the doors opened to the penthouse level. He led her down the marble hallway and then opened the door to his East-facing unit.

"This is beautiful. It looks like the kind of place where you'd live."

He stood back and let her wander, her big curious eyes taking in the post-modern furniture his decorator had picked out and the artwork on the walls that he'd bought sight unseen. Her words, innocent as they were, pierced through straight to his newly exposed underbelly.

He'd lived there for years and it still didn't feel like home. More like a place to rest his head on the random days when he didn't crash in his office. Suddenly, it was like he could see himself through her eyes and he didn't like what he saw.

A man who worked at the expense of everything else in his life.

A man who prioritized business deals over even his own well-being.

When was the last time he'd done anything that didn't further the business interests of Kingsley International? He honestly couldn't think of one thing.

Damn, he was tired.

Suddenly he wanted to be anywhere else. This place had no real meaning to him and irrationally, he didn't want Olivia tainted by its coldness.

"I hate everything about this place," he muttered.

Surprise registered in her eyes but then she glanced away. The silence stretched out, a taut wire that could easily snap and maim them both.

"I'm sorry I didn't call you."

She kept her eyes on the floor. "I'm sure you were busy. So was I."

"That wasn't why I didn't call. It was because I didn't want to. I don't like the way I feel when I'm with you."

That got her attention. She dropped her bag on the couch and faced him for the first time.

"You are such an ass. What did I ever do to you?"

He walked a little closer, feeling like he was taking his life in his hands. If the daggers coming from her eyes got any closer he'd be bleeding from every orifice.

"You did plenty to me, angel. You got in my head so I couldn't concentrate at work. The scent of you lingered on everything you touched and taunted me for weeks. I washed everything I wore that night and still couldn't escape it. Finally I gave in and wrapped the shirt I wore around my dick and stroked one out while pretending you were watching."

Her throat moved as she swallowed, her cheeks flushing pink at his words.

"You're crude," she accused but her eyes were bright, betraying her arousal at his words.

"Did you think of me all this time angel? Put those dainty little fingers in your pussy while pretending I was fucking you?"

She beat against his chest and then moaned when he grabbed her arms and held her against his chest. Unable to resist any longer, his mouth found her throat and he held there, breathing against her skin.

"I hate you," she whispered.

"No, you don't. I almost wish you did. I'm not the guy for you, Olivia. You've always been honest about what you think of me. Arrogant. Entitled. And you're absolutely right. I'm nowhere near good enough for you but I want you anyway."

He grasped her hair and speared his fingers through it, pulling out the low bun her long curls had been bundled into. Then he covered her mouth with his, not waiting for her to catch up to his intensity. She gasped for breath in between kisses, her hands clasping the front of his shirt as if desperate for something to anchor her in the midst of this storm of desire.

Her taste was everything he'd been missing and already he was hard and thick, ready to give her what they both needed. But this time he'd go slowly, lick her all over her delectable little body and then keep her on the edge of orgasm for hours before he finally let her go.

Then she suddenly pushed him away.

"No. This isn't happening again."

Stunned, King reached for her and then dropped his hands when she glared at him. Chuckling, he put his hands on top of his head to keep them out of grabbing distance.

"That was too fast, I agree. I promised I would do it right this time. Take it slow. You make me a greedy man, Olivia."

Although her eyes heated at his words, she planted a firm hand on his chest when he tried to move closer.

"No. You're still not listening. I don't want this. Maybe my body wants this but I'm not a toy you can pick up when you're bored and ready to play, King."

The characterization bothered him. King knew he wasn't the most nurturing man. He was used to getting exactly what he wanted, exactly when he wanted it. But he'd never thought of himself as a user. It made him feel like he was just one more person who didn't appreciate her.

Or worse, someone who actively dimmed her shine.

He remembered how she'd wilted under her father's careless words earlier that night. He never wanted to see her look like that again.

"I'm in unfamiliar territory here. I want you to stay and I have no idea how to get you to want that, too."

She laughed but it was a bitter sound.

"Welcome to what life is like for the rest of us. *Newsflash*, you don't always get what you want. I have the right to protect myself here. I need more than just a screw against a bedroom wall. You don't. It seems pretty clear to me that I'm the one who'd get hurt. Would you take a chance on a risky investment, Mr. Businessman?"

She had a point. But he didn't think of this thing between them as a bad investment. He wanted her, more than he'd ever wanted another woman. Not just for sex either. He wanted to talk to her and get her unique perspective on things. He wanted to know she was safe, even when he couldn't be with her.

He wanted to see her smile.

He wanted to make her happy.

King realized with not just a little bit of horror, that what he was describing resembled something he'd avoided for years. A relationship. He wanted a relationship with Olivia.

And she didn't trust him at all.

"If I was willing to try for more, would you give me a chance?"

Olivia sighed. "That's not how it works, King. You can't just pretend to care for a while."

"I've never pretended with you, angel. I've never felt like this before. I want to see you every day. When I go to sleep at night, the last thing I think about is you. I'm not sure what the hell that means but I think it means... I want more, too."

She stared at him, a flicker of surprise crossing her face before she smirked. "You wouldn't know what more looked like if it bit you in the ass."

"You're right. I'm probably going to be a crap boyfriend. But maybe you might like crap? Hell, that's not how I meant that to come out. You know what I meant."

Her shoulders shook with silent laughter. She was so damn cute he took a chance and pulled her in for a soft kiss. Her giggles subsided and she gazed up at him with an unfamiliar expression, one that looked a lot like hope.

"I know I've let you down before but I'm going to prove I'm serious about you. Will you let me try?"

She sighed. "Okay. I want to see what more looks like on you."

He took a chance and traced the edges of her lips. She had a beautiful smile and he hoped he would get to see a lot more of it. He was suddenly beset with anxiety. Everything was riding on him proving his worth and he had no idea how to do that.

Olivia snuggled closer and the hand on his chest worked it's way down to cup the still-hard bulge between his legs. She squeezed gently, smiling in triumph when he groaned. It took willpower he didn't know he had to step back, putting about a foot of space between them.

Her eyes rounded. "You don't want to?"

"Oh, I want to. But I'm going to prove to you that I'm serious. Which means, the only thing I'm going to do to that delectable little ass of yours right now is drive it home."

Her shock was almost worth the case of blue-balls he was sure to have later that night.

Almost.

———

*O*livia invited King inside but he declined, surprising her yet again. Although he'd turned her down back at his place, she didn't actually think he'd have the willpower to do it twice. Especially since they'd gotten each other pretty worked up before he'd called a halt to things.

There was a tentative knock on the door. Olivia rolled her eyes. Just as she'd thought. He'd changed his mind already. She hadn't even gotten her coat off. How predictable.

She yanked the door open. "I thought you said you wanted to prove yourself?"

The girl on the other side of the threshold slowly lowered her hand where it had been poised to knock again. "Expecting someone else?"

It had been a few weeks but Olivia never forgot a face.

"Georgina? What are you doing here?"

She shifted from foot to foot and then glanced over her shoulder. "Do you mind if I come in? It's kind of a long story."

"Of course. Come in."

Olivia stepped back and allowed Georgina to squeeze past her into the entryway. She hung up both of their coats on the pegs behind the door and then motioned for Georgina to follow her.

"Come on. I'll make us some coffee."

Georgina sat on one of the barstools at the breakfast bar and looked around curiously. "I like your place. This is just the kind of place I'd want if I lived on my own."

"You still live with your parents? I didn't realize."

Georgina made a face. "They never want me to do anything on my own. They're so overprotective. Now that Alex has proposed," she held up her left hand which sported a diamond the size of a small boulder, "I'll probably just go straight from living in their house to his."

She sounded so resigned about it. Olivia hadn't met her fiance at the party, not that she remembered, but it sounded like Georgina wasn't too happy with him.

"It sounds like he's eager to have you with him."

Georgina's shoulders drooped. "Yes, he is. That's what makes this so much harder. I'm sorry to come here and dump this on you but I didn't know who else to talk to.

Alex and I have too many friends in common. But if King trusts you, then I know I can, too."

Olivia gripped the side of the counter. She hated to lie but she couldn't exactly tell Georgina that she wasn't really King's girlfriend.

Crap.

"Um, well, I'm not sure I'll have any advice for you. I'm not close with my family the way you are with yours. So I've been on my own for a long time."

Why was the coffee taking so long? Olivia looked at the machine and prayed for it to percolate a little faster. She'd entertain Georgina for a while and then make an excuse so she could text King and ask what he wanted her to do. This wasn't part of their original ruse and she didn't think he'd appreciate her getting involved in his family's personal affairs.

The coffee continued to produce a minuscule trickle.

Olivia groaned and sent Georgina an apologetic look. "Sorry this coffeemaker is so slow. It's kind of ancient."

Georgina smiled. "Why hasn't King just bought you a new one? I never thought my brother would need lessons on how to keep a woman."

"I don't need your brother to buy me anything. Just because we're... together doesn't mean he's my sugar daddy. I take care of myself. I have for a long time."

Georgina's face fell. "I'm so sorry, Olivia. I didn't mean anything by that, I swear."

Now she just felt like a bully.

Olivia hung her head. "I know you didn't. Sorry to jump down your throat. That's kind of a sore spot with me. People always assume I need a man to do certain things. But I've always been independent."

"I'm so glad you said that because that's why I'm here. I've never been independent. Between my parents and Alex, I feel like I'm suffocating. There are so many things I can't talk about with them and I've never been free to try anything on my own."

She glanced over at Olivia and then whispered, "I have a confession to make. After King brought you home that day, I did a little digging."

Olivia's stomach dropped. *Oh shit.*

"Georgina–"

"Call me Georgie. I really hope we'll be good friends."

The deflection reminded her so much of King she couldn't help smiling. Both of the Kingsley siblings were definitely used to getting what they wanted, when they wanted it.

"You're not used to taking no for an answer, are you?"

"Nope. That's why I hope you won't be mad when I tell you I know all about Club VIP. I was hoping you could get me a membership there."

Shit. Shit. Double shit.

"I don't know about that, Georgie. King would be so angry if he found out I did this behind his back."

"Why is it about him? Women need to be independent, isn't that what you said? I've only ever had sex with one person! In my whole life. I love Alex, I really do. But..."

Now she looked like she was on the verge of tears. Olivia didn't need to be that intuitive to understand what she wasn't saying. She knew Georgie's life all too well. Always being the good girl while burying any desires you had that fell outside of what society considered proper.

"I'm going to regret helping you. I already know I am. But I'm going to do it anyway."

Georgie squealed and threw her arms around Olivia's neck. "Thank you! I won't do anything crazy, I promise. I just want to know more about what's out there. Isn't it better to go where I know I'll be safe?"

"It is. That's the main reason I'm doing this. But there are going to be some rules. Don't do anything on impulse. Also, I have to know when you'll be there so I can make sure no one bothers you."

Georgie nodded eagerly. "This is so exciting. I promise I just want the chance to live a little before I'm all married and boring and stuff."

Olivia choked back a laugh. "Okay. I guess I can understand that."

"Don't worry about the coffee. I'm going home and getting into bed. See, I'm already boring."

Olivia saw her out and then went back to the kitchen to turn off the coffeemaker. After a quick shower, she climbed in bed. She opened her clutch to get her cellphone and inside, found a note in a bold, masculine scrawl.

Sleep well, angel.

Damn him. They hadn't even started dating yet and she was already won over.

This was going to end badly. She was going to fall for him and a man like King didn't know how to be true. Dating was a game to him, a challenge he'd never conquered. He was used to women giving him what he wanted and she was the only one who was willing to tell him to go fuck himself.

As much fun as she was having playing this game with him, she had to remember that it was just that. A game.

If she wasn't careful, she was the one who'd end up getting played.

Chapter 11

Olivia hadn't been sure what to expect the first week. Wealthy men usually wanted to show off, trying to buy your affection with expensive trips or gifts. But despite what King thought, he actually turned out to be a pretty good boyfriend.

On their first official date, King showed up with a single rose and took her out for dinner at a local steakhouse. It was probably miles below the kind of places he was used to but he'd seemed completely at ease. Afterward they'd gone to a performance of *A MidSummer Night's Dream* at a small theatre she'd never even known was in the city.

The entire night she'd expected him to make a move, put his hand on her knee or grab her ass. But other than holding her hand and a perfectly chaste kiss on the forehead, he hadn't touched her at all. Their next two dates had been more of the same except he kissed her for real on the third night.

Finally she understood what he was doing. He was trying to court her in the most old-fashioned way possible. At least he hadn't brought a chaperone!

It was a little more than what she'd expected but Olivia thought it was kind of cute. King wasn't the sort of man who was used to having to prove himself. The fact that he was willing to do it for her was no small thing.

On their fourth date, King came over with a bag of takeout. "I thought we could stay in and watch something on Netflix."

Olivia grinned. Everyone knew what that meant. Staying in and watching movies was code for *let's get busy on the couch.* She was more than ready.

Their dates had been such a surprise, showing her that there were hidden depths to the man she'd always thought of as a cold automaton. But after a week of look but don't touch, she was just about ready to jump him.

"Sounds good to me."

He set up everything on her coffee table while she brought them beers. It hadn't been a conscious thing but she'd found herself buying his favorite brand of beer when she was at the store the prior day. It hadn't even sunk in until she'd gotten home and put the case in the refrigerator.

Don't make it a big deal. So you bought his favorite beer. That's just being nice.

"I hope beef and broccoli is okay?"

Olivia accepted the small white carton gratefully. King's hand enclosed hers, his thumb tracing over the thin white scar that ran all the way up her arm.

"What happened here?"

She debated just making something up or ignoring the question but then she just went with the truth.

"I was in a car accident."

He rubbed the slightly raised flesh gently. "I'm sorry. I didn't mean to bring up a bad memory."

"It's not your fault. It was just a rough time in my life."

She looked up to find King watching her intently. In that moment, she'd never felt closer to anyone. It made her want to confide in him, tell him all the things that had ever scared her so he could slay the dragons and carry her off to his castle. The image made her smile.

"Maybe it's good it left a scar. It reminds me that if I could go through that alone and make it out intact, then I'm strong enough to do anything."

"Alone? Where was your family?"

Olivia put her carton of food back on the table. This was a make or break moment. She didn't talk about that time in her life not because she was ashamed of the choices she'd made but because it was so intensely personal. Even after all these years, her emotions were still raw when it came to the accident and all that she'd lost.

"My father kicked me out when I was nineteen. I was pregnant."

King's arm tightened around her. He was a smart man and after they'd spent so much time together she knew he could intuit that this story didn't have a happy ending.

"My father is very conservative. His parents came here from Cuba with nothing but the clothes on their backs and their faith. Catholics don't tend to be okay with their daughters getting pregnant out of wedlock. I told them about the baby almost as soon as I found out myself. I was so scared. Back then, that was what I did when something scared me. I ran to Mommy and Daddy."

"What happened, angel?"

Tears welled in her eyes and she paused for a second, taking a moment to compose herself.

"My best friend Bennett saved me. He let me stay with him even though his apartment was tiny. I got a job working at a clothing boutique and worked as much as I could to save up money. I have a trust fund but I would have rather chewed glass than take anything from my father after the things he said to me. Then one night, I was driving home from closing the shop and ... I fell asleep."

King pressed a soft kiss to the top of her head. "I am so sorry, Olivia."

She shrugged, trying to shake off the fresh wave of sadness and guilt. "It's a time in my life that I try not to think about anymore. My pride cost me everything. My baby would have been going to kindergarten this year."

At that she totally lost it. She covered her face with her hands and just cried.

King pulled her until she was sprawled across his lap and she clutched his shirt in her fists until the wracking sobs slowed and she could catch her breath. His hands traveled up and down her back in a gentle circular motion and for about ten minutes they stayed just like that. A wave of exhaustion passed through Olivia but it was a good kind of tired.

It felt like a weight had been lifted.

Finally she sat back and brushed at the tears on her cheek. King's shirt was creased and covered in dark spots where her tears had soaked through. Self-conscious at the signs of her breakdown, she slid off his lap and onto the couch cushion next to him.

"Sorry about that. When I invited you over, I'm sure you weren't expecting to play therapist."

King brushed her cheek with his thumb and leaned down so she couldn't avoid his eyes. "When I told you that I was serious, I didn't just mean when it was convenient. I don't mind listening to anything you want to share with me."

Her heart rolled over in her chest and Olivia lowered her head so he wouldn't see the cheesy smile on her face. Before today she would have said that she was enjoying her time with King but it wasn't until this very moment that she started to think he might be more than just a fun time.

That he might actually be the kind of man that she could count on.

Forever.

———

*K*ing flipped the pen in his hands over and over. His mind wasn't on the financial statements strewn across his desk or whatever the hell his CFO was saying. Olivia had sent him a text asking him to meet her at Club VIP and his mind had been on the possibilities all day.

Ever since the day Olivia had told him about her accident, there had been an entirely different vibe between them. He understood so many things about her better now. Her strength, her courage, her determination to do everything on her own. She'd lost so much but still had such a positive spirit.

Spending time with her had been such a surprise. In the past whenever he spent time with a woman, it had quickly become routine. The women in his usual social circle all seemed to talk about the same things and the same people. Their worldview was limited to what they could buy or who they could be seen with. King was no better, he'd come to realize because he hadn't picked his partners for their wit or intelligence. He'd only cared about getting the hottest women who wouldn't care when he inevitably got bored and moved on.

With Olivia, he never knew what was going to happen. If there was a news story she found interesting they would end up debating it. When she'd told him a local conservative group was trying to get the club shut down, they'd brainstormed ways to handle it. She was interested in his business and asked questions that showed she cared about how he spent his days.

Best of all, he had no doubt that even if he was a garbage man she'd give him the same level of support and interest. She wasn't interested in Kingsley International or how powerful he was due to his position there. She cared about *him*.

Her support was quickly becoming vital to his wellbeing.

King's attention was diverted when Devin stood.

"I'll have an answer for you next week. Until then, I'll get with legal and see what's necessary."

James, who had also been invited to the meeting, frowned at him before saying something to the other man and walking with him to the door. King sighed and glanced at his watch. It would be at least another two hours before he could get out of here and meet Olivia.

"Did you hear anything he said?" James demanded. He rapped his knuckles on the desk between them and glared at King. "You've been somewhere else all afternoon. What the hell is going on with you?"

King wasn't used to having his authority questioned but his oldest friend was one of the only people who didn't mince words with him. They'd been through too much and seen each other in too many compromising positions over the years to stand on ceremony.

"No, I didn't. I'm sure you've got it covered."

The statement reminded him of something his father had said to him not that long ago. He'd probably been wearing the same disgusted look his best friend was currently sporting afterward.

Maybe his father was actually on to something. This delegating thing wasn't so bad.

James leaned forward. "Is this about a woman?"

Uncomfortable now, King avoided his eyes and shuffled the papers on his desk unnecessarily. Ever since that night at the club, he hadn't mentioned his plan to James again. Usually they didn't keep secrets but he wasn't entirely sure how to explain what he was doing with Olivia.

They'd been dating for the past few weeks and everything was great but how long could that really last?

He wasn't the kind of guy who could stay on the straight and narrow but for so long, something that James knew better than anyone else. He didn't want to hear his friend's opinions on his attempt at being less of an asshole.

It was immature but he was enjoying being in this bubble of happiness with Olivia. While they were together he could believe that things would always stay this way between them and that he could have a chance at what he'd always mocked his friends for wanting.

"Everything is fine. Come on, you know as well as I do that Devin analyzes everything to death before making any recommendations anyway. I'm sure whatever I need to know is in here in great detail." He gestured toward the financial statements Devin had been talking them through.

James didn't look convinced but he didn't seem inclined to dig any deeper. He stood and rebuttoned his suit jacket. Right before he reached the door, he stopped.

"Hey, I've been meaning to ask you something. Is Georgie okay?"

That got his attention. His friends teased him about his overprotective big brother mode but he didn't care. Georgie had been sheltered her whole life and she needed looking after. Even now that she was engaged, his mind refused to acknowledge her as anything other than a freckle-faced toddler with pigtails. It had taken him ages to warm up to her fiancé and he still wasn't sure the guy was worthy.

"Why wouldn't she be? Did she say something to you?"

"No, of course not. I dropped some files off for your father at home and ran into her. She looked upset."

"She hasn't said anything to me."

The thought bothered him as did the thought that James might have noticed something wrong with her before he did.

He'd never told his best friend this before but he suspected that Georgie used to have a crush on him at one point. Anyone else wouldn't have noticed the signs but King knew his little sister. She was usually excited and full of energy and whenever James would come around she was suddenly quiet and demure, like she was trying too hard to look unaffected.

"I'll check on her tonight."

James hesitated, as if deciding whether he wanted to say anything else. But in the end, he just nodded and left, pulling the office door closed behind him.

There was more to this story, King could sense that. But the thought of it made him uncomfortable so he decided that he would take a little detour and visit Georgie before going home. He'd get the truth out of her. He didn't want James getting involved.

The last thing he needed was to worry about his best friend anywhere near his baby sister.

Chapter 12

Olivia pulled the curtain around the stage and stood back to inspect her handiwork. A last minute cancellation had come through that morning and she'd immediately thought of King.

It usually took quite a bit of juggling to get a two hour block of time to use the Masquerade Room, even on a weeknight.

She supposed that was a blessing though. The room was becoming more popular with the patrons of the club and they actually had a waiting list for every weekend through the end of the summer.

She was hit with a sudden case of nerves at the thought of being on stage in front of him. In the past she'd never wanted to dance for a lover, preferring to keep that part of her life separate. But with King, she felt like she could share every part of herself, from her fears to her most intense and intimate desires.

He had a way of making her feel like anything they did together couldn't be wrong. They'd gotten so close these past few weeks and she'd wanted to do something for him.

More than that, she *really* wanted to seduce him.

After she'd cried all over him during their last date, he'd been so sweet. They'd eaten Chinese food while watching the first few episodes of a new sitcom neither of them had ever seen. Afterward, he'd carried her to her room and made slow, sweet love to her.

It was hard to believe sometimes that the man who handled her with such sensitivity and care was the same man who'd once made her work life a living hell. But as much as she appreciated how gentle and understanding he'd been, especially after telling him about her accident, she kind of wanted to push him a little.

Their passion had always been off the charts and she could just feel him holding himself back. Well, she didn't want the watered down version of King. She wanted every part of him, including the dominant, wild, out of control aggressive lover he'd been in the beginning.

Her phone vibrated in the pocket of the silk robe she wore. She pulled it out and read the message from Andrew, the head of security for Club VIP.

King was here.

By the time he entered a few minutes later, she was in position on the stage, her back to the pole. The music she'd chosen was playing at full volume. She'd even turned on the strobe lights and it lent a sultry almost seedy atmosphere to the setting.

He wore the standard black eye mask provided outside of the room, as did she. She shivered as his eyes ran over her hungrily.

"Is the room set up to your liking, Mr. Kingsley."

His eyes flashed at her reference to how they'd originally met. "Actually, I have a few suggestions."

"Such as," she taunted.

"Lose the robe."

She untied the sash around her waist and allowed the robe to slide down and pool around her feet, revealing her purple tasseled bra and thong. King settled on the couch directly facing the stage, his hands resting lightly on his knees.

Olivia rolled her hips to the beat of the music and leaned back against the pole, using it to steady her as she gyrated. King's hands clenched into fists when she wrapped one leg around the pole and leaned back, popping her hips like she was grinding against the metal. She used her ab muscles to pull herself upright in one long sensuous motion and then jumped, grabbing the pole and inverting herself as she swung around the pole slowly.

The flashing colors of the strobe lights added to the surreal feeling, making Olivia feel like she was flying. Using the strength in her legs, she allowed herself to slide down to the floor and then flipped her legs over her head, until she was on all fours on the stage.

She kept her eyes on King as she crawled slowly toward him. He was sitting all the way forward on the couch and looked like he was about two seconds away from falling off. She crooked her finger at him and he sprang forward.

He hadn't changed after work but he'd removed his suit jacket and she could clearly see how her performance had affected him.

"Holy shit, Liv. That was amazing."

She got up on her knees and hooked a finger underneath the knot of his tie, tugging him closer. He groaned and came down on top of her, his mouth grinding against hers roughly. She welcomed it, wanted him completely out of control.

They rolled on the stage, pulling at each other's clothes until she was topless and his shirt was hanging half off. King pulled back slightly and then yanked his shirt off the rest of the way. Olivia ran her hands over his chest and tugged at his belt. She giggled when he pushed her hands out of the way and almost ripped it off.

"This is funny, is it Miss Reyes?"

She nodded but was no longer laughing when he turned her over so she was bent over the edge of the stage. He tugged at her thong, helping her step out of it. His hands tangled in her hair, pulling her back as he ground his erection against her ass.

"Maybe I should spank you for teasing me," he murmured.

Olivia's belly clenched and she could feel how wet she was by how her thighs were slipping against each other. When his fingers left her hair, she moaned softly then cried out when his mouth feathered over the skin on her ass. He spanked her right ass cheek and she bit her lip, tasting the sharp tang of blood.

"Hold still. Don't you dare move."

She cried out when his tongue slicked over her, sucking gently. It was impossible to hold still while he slowly licked her to heaven but Olivia didn't even care because every time he smacked her ass it just heightened the pleasure. Her orgasm unfurled in a slow, rolling wave of pleasure. When she emerged back to reality, she heard the rip of foil, then felt him enter her with a deep thrust.

Gone was the hesitant, gentle lover she'd come to know. This was her arrogant, demanding bad King.

In this position she was taking him deeper than before and the new angle hit spots that made her dizzy. He pulled her up, running his hands over her belly and the tips of her breasts, stimulating her in new and different ways. Olivia couldn't keep up with all the ways he was touching her, his hands now on her hips, his lips on her ear, his thick cock stroking inside her.

His fingers flexed on her hips as he came, shouting out his pleasure just as another orgasm rolled through her. For a long moment afterward they stayed just like that, motionless as the last aftershocks of release drained out of them both.

Finally King kissed her on the side of the neck and pulled out gently. "You're going to kill me. I'm getting too old for this."

She chuckled, knowing he was only five years older than she was. Hardly an old man.

"Should I take it easy on you, then?"

"Oh no. If I'm going to die, this is how I want to go. Strobe lights, pole dancing and all."

Olivia hit him on the arm. "Now that's the King I know."

They dressed in comfortable silence. King managed to make his suit look presentable despite missing half the buttons on his shirt while Olivia changed back into the dress she'd worn to the club.

She was glad she'd taken a previously booked time slot because it meant she didn't have to clean the room herself. Club VIP staff would clean and rearrange the room just as if there had been a member event.

"Let's go home."

It wasn't until they were in the car that Olivia wondered what he'd meant by that. Her home? His home? She wasn't sure what he meant since after all of their dates, he'd never slept over. She didn't want to push him.

It was a big step for someone like King and truthfully for her, too.

In the car on the way home her phone vibrated in her purse. When she saw Georgie's name, she glanced over at King. Since his eyes were fixed on the road, she right-swiped to read the text.

- Is this a good night for me to visit VIP?

Olivia bit her lip. She'd already warned security she had a special guest who was going to visit the club and made sure she was on the all-access list. Andrew had agreed to keep an eye out and make sure all the bouncers were aware that Georgie was a VIP. She wasn't worried about her safety at all.

But would King see it the same way when he found out? She wasn't fooling herself they'd be able to keep it a secret forever.

Olivia sighed and sent a message to Andrew to give him a heads up and then texted Georgie back.

- All clear.

It made her feel so guilty to deceive King but she couldn't imagine only having sex with one person ever. Had the girl even had an orgasm? That was no way to live. She was sure King would understand once she explained everything. Who knew, maybe Georgie would visit one time and decide she hated it.

Maybe King never had to know.

———

Whenever King brought a woman to his place in the past, it usually wasn't long before he found their company exhausting. They'd ask too many questions or make themselves a little *too* comfortable. It was why he'd never had a live-in girlfriend. He didn't figure there was any point since he would inevitably reach that point when he wanted his space.

With Olivia, that moment never came.

She'd been subdued when they first arrived at his place. There were times he got the sense she was uncomfortable with his wealth. Downstairs in the garage he'd noticed her staring at the Bentley. It wasn't something he knew how to address.

Usually he was trying to fend off women who wanted to know more about what he was worth but with Olivia, the things that mattered to her were emotional not monetary.

It was something he'd have to keep an eye on but once they got upstairs she was back to her usual happy self.

"Hungry, baby?"

"Actually, I am. We worked up quite an appetite."

He chuckled and pulled out the menu for the local Italian place. Olivia loved Italian food as much as he did. He ordered baked ziti, lasagna and a new risotto dish just because. The food arrived quickly and they ate at the small dining table he rarely used.

Afterward, Olivia stretched out on the couch. He sat next to her and pulled her slender feet onto his lap. It seemed like such a natural thing to have her here while the day wound down, her musical laugh accompanying his favorite late night sitcom. She fit so fluidly into his life, as if she'd always been there.

The more he had of her, the more he wanted. He was coming to realize it would probably always be that way. She was a complicated, loving, exasperating woman and no matter how long he knew her, he'd never have time to undercover the many facets of who she was. Olivia Reyes was a puzzle he'd never solve. One he never wanted to solve. He enjoyed being surprised by her everyday.

"Stay."

She glanced over at him and raised her eyebrows in confusion.

He cleared his throat. "Will you stay with me tonight?"

She didn't ask why now or show any outward sign that she recognized this was a huge step for him. He braced himself for her to make a big deal out of it or for her to suddenly want to talk about things. But Olivia just leaned over and kissed him on the cheek.

"Okay."

And that was when he knew he was in serious trouble.

Chapter 13

Olivia woke feeling like there was something she was forgetting. Then she opened her eyes and realized why.

She wasn't at home.

She was at King's place.

It shouldn't feel so validating that he'd wanted her to sleep over.

Seeing someone at night was a bigger deal than most people gave it credit for. When you were tired, you were at your most vulnerable. The makeup came off, the comfy clothes went on and your guard went down. You could tell a lot about a person by the way they shared their bed.

King was a cuddler.

Olivia smiled into her pillow. She didn't think he was awake yet because his arm was still securely wrapped around her waist and she could feel the even rhythm of his chest rising and falling at her back. This was perfect, to wake warm and safe all wrapped up like she was his most precious treasure.

Even if it wasn't true, she was going to wallow in the moment for just a little longer. Until reality woke them both up.

Unfortunately, her plans to wallow were trumped by her intense need for the bathroom. Carefully extricating herself from his arms, she tiptoed to the door on the other side of the room. After taking care of business, she washed her hands, brushed her teeth and splashed her face with water. She was all for reality but no one needed to see her with her zombie face on.

When she opened the door, King was sitting up in bed.

"Hey, I hope I didn't wake you."

The morning light illuminated the room and somehow, King looked even better first thing in the morning. The sheet had slipped low on his waist putting his spectacular chest on display. With his lean muscles, arrogant smirk and just-fucked dark hair going in every direction, he looked like a billboard advertising bad decisions.

Olivia regretted nothing.

She climbed back in bed and pulled the covers up to her chin. "I was planning on getting back in bed and being very lazy this morning."

It occurred to her then that even though he'd invited her to sleep over, he might have other plans for today. She didn't want to ever be *that girl*, the one who couldn't take a hint and overstayed her welcome.

She sat up and ran a hand through her hair. "But now that I'm awake, I should probably get going. There's a million things I need to do today."

She could feel his eyes on her as she climbed out of bed and leaned down to grab the dress she'd worn the night before. It was all smashed and wrinkled but it would have to do. She didn't even care who saw her.

It was doubtful she was the first girl to do the walk of shame out of this building.

King leaned over and snatched the dress out of her hands.

"What are you doing?"

He threw it over his shoulder and then grabbed her around the waist, twisting them so they fell together on top of the covers.

"I'm making sure you don't have anything to wear. Then you have to stay with me."

"You're keeping me prisoner, now?"

He kissed her all over her face until her stomach hurt from laughing. She would have never guessed he was so playful in the morning.

"I would love to keep you prisoner but I'm hungry. Maybe we can play pirate after we go out for breakfast."

Olivia frowned. She hadn't expected to go out for breakfast. They'd just ordered out last night. It was a small thing but if they were going to give it a shot, she was going to have to accept that he was insanely wealthy.

It made her uncomfortable but it wasn't going to change. He was used to pressing a button and having exactly what he wanted delivered. He was used to paying people to do things for him.

He'd toned down his arrogance a lot since they'd been together but it would likely always be a part of him. She didn't believe in changing a man, you either loved him as he already was or not at all.

But that didn't mean she couldn't be a good influence on him.

"Why don't I cook us breakfast? It's faster which means we can come back to bed faster." She squealed when he leaned down to blow kisses on her belly.

"That sounds amazing. I can't cook otherwise I'd help. But it's probably best for everyone's safety if I stay out of the kitchen."

She walked over to the other side of the bed and retrieved her dress. After yanking it over her head, she winked at him.

"Uh huh. That sounds like a really convenient excuse to get out of doing any work. But I'll let you slide this time."

"Just–" King stopped when his phone rang.

They both looked around trying to identify where it was coming from. Olivia eventually found it in the closet in the pocket of his suit jacket but the call had already gone to voicemail.

"Thank you, angel. It's probably just my parents or something."

She kissed him on the forehead. "You handle that and then come out to the kitchen when you're ready. I plan on eating fast."

His laugh followed her as she left the room.

———

When King saw he had fifteen missed calls, his brain immediately went into crisis mode. Not that many people had his personal cell phone number and none of them were stupid enough to blow up his phone without good cause.

His worry lessened only slightly when he saw all of the calls were from James. He sighed. The deal they'd been working on must have hit a snag. Over the past few weeks he'd delegated more and more work to James and his friend had covered for him. However, he couldn't continue to live in his Olivia-bubble forever.

Especially if something had gone wrong with the AliCorp deal.

"James. What's up?"

"I need you to promise you won't lose it."

King wasn't in the mood for games. James had a tendency to make every situation into a fire. He usually just let him talk and get it out of his system but he usually didn't have a beautiful woman in his kitchen cooking him breakfast. If it was a competition between his friend's weekly bitch session and eating breakfast with Olivia, there was no contest.

"Just tell me what the hell is going on?"

James groaned. "It's about Georgie."

"What do you mean? Is she okay? Where is she?"

King could hear the growl in his own voice. Damn it, he'd been so self-involved lately that he hadn't pushed his sister to tell him what was wrong. If something had happened to her because he was so wrapped up in Olivia he would never forgive himself.

"She's fine and she's at home, now."

There was a curious emphasis on the last word that caught King's attention. "What do you mean *now*? Where was she before?"

James sighed. "I found her wandering around Club VIP. I almost didn't recognize her at first. She was dressed... differently."

King couldn't hear anything after that, the blood rushing to his head so fast he had an instant headache.

His sister had been at Club VIP?

Not only did that introduce mental images that made him want to bleach his brain but it also made him wonder how the hell she'd known about the club? Was it possible that Georgie had followed him there? It was too big of a coincidence to be believed.

He bent over and put his head between his knees. Had his sister paid for a membership to Club VIP also? She'd come into her trust fund once she hit twenty-one so she could definitely afford it. Or was this done at her fiance's request?

King ground his teeth.

Was the bastard forcing his sister to accompany him while he looked at strippers? He knew it was contradictory since he and James frequented the club but he'd never claimed to be a good guy. He sure as hell didn't want his sister with a guy like him. She deserved way better than that.

"I'm going to kill Alex," he snapped into the phone. "Find that fucker and let me know where he is."

"Um, King? Alex wasn't with her. Not that I saw anyway. It was just Georgie. Wandering around the Fantasy Room wearing this low-cut–"

"James!"

"Sorry. I didn't... Whatever, the point is she was there alone. I don't think Alex knows anything about this because she asked me not to tell anyone. She definitely didn't want me to tell you."

"Of course she didn't want you to tell me because she knows she shouldn't have been there! Look, I'll take care of everything. I'll talk to Georgie and find out what the hell is going on. She probably saw us going there or heard something about it and didn't know what kind of place it was."

"Right. But I just have one question," James interjected, catching King right before he would have hung up.

In his mind, now that he understood the problem, he was ready to tackle the solution. Number one on his list, procure a chastity belt to keep his little sister safe from the perverts of the world.

"What's that?"

"When I first found her, she kept saying it was okay because Olivia knew she was there. She was three sheets to the wind so I could only understand half of what she was saying. But I'm still not sure what that means. Who the hell is Olivia?"

King's mouth fell open. "She said *Olivia* told her about the club?"

"Yeah, I guess. That's what it sounded like. Who is that anyway?"

"Fuck!"

King almost threw the phone. All this time he'd assumed Olivia was so different, that she wasn't the type to scheme or plot. Now he found out the entire time she'd been cozying up to his sister and worse, pulling her into things Georgie was in no way equipped to handle.

If she thought being BFFs with his sister was the way to get him to settle down then she'd miscalculated.

"Do you remember that night at Club VIP? When I said I'd found my bride?"

"Wait, you actually went through with that?"

James didn't say anything but King could just imagine what he was thinking. That King had been led around by the nose by a woman who was probably manipulating him *and* his sister.

The thought sent his blood pressure through the roof.

"So she's the reason you've been so distracted lately?" James didn't bother to conceal his annoyance.

"Yes, James. This is what we need to worry about right now, that I've been fucking a stripper hoping to piss off my parents." Sarcasm dripped from his voice. "Look, I'll take care of this. This is my problem. But there's no way I'm going to have Georgie's reputation ruined because someone sees her at some trashy club."

"Got it. But King don't expect Georgie to be happy to see you. She was pretty pissed when I pulled her out of there last night."

"I bet she was."

King looked up and his fingers clenched around the phone. Olivia stood in the doorway, a spatula in her hand and devastation written across her face.

"James, I have to go."

He hung up but didn't move otherwise. There was no reason to ask how much she'd heard because her face told the whole story. Regret wrapped him up like a hand around his throat but just as quickly he pushed the sensation away. She was the one who'd lied and schemed behind his back.

He looked away. Olivia's soft sniffle carried across the room to where he sat as if he was right next to her.

"Your eggs are ready." She dropped the spatula that she held and left the room.

King didn't move when she walked away. He held still as the front door slammed. He didn't even move when his phone rang again about ten minutes later.

He stayed in that position for a long time, trying in vain to feel anything at all.

Chapter 14

For the next few days, Olivia went about her regular routine as if nothing had changed. She went to work, she went to the gym and she came home and went to bed.

Even when a member complained because she'd taken down the wrong theme for their event, Olivia couldn't muster the energy to care. Her emotions had just shut down completely.

She was scared to care about anything because then her heart would have to accept that she was in love with an asshole.

As she walked into the elevator at Club VIP, she took a deep breath. What the hell was she supposed to do now? It hurt so much to find out that King was using her as... what? A chance to see if Latina girls were as spicy as he'd heard? Slumming it with a girl he saw as no better than "the help"?

How could she have been so utterly wrong about him?

Then there was the matter of Bennett. He'd left her a message confirming that he'd see her that weekend for the Mentor Science award ceremony. In the midst of everything that had happened, she'd totally forgotten about it.

That was probably a blessing in disguise. She'd been so stupidly in love with King that she would have canceled her date with Bennett if she'd remembered. Even though she would never be the kind of woman who ditched her friends just because she had a boyfriend, she wouldn't have felt right going to the dinner with Bennett if she was seriously involved with someone.

Now it didn't matter.

She should be happy. Now that King had shown his true colors, she could focus on her date with Bennett, the perfect guy.

But how could she when she couldn't stop thinking about *Mr. Totally Wrong for Her?*

Olivia stopped in front of the doors leading to the street. What was the point of even going home right now? She might as well hang out a little longer, maybe have a drink. She doubled back and used her access key to take the elevator to the third floor of the club. Regina nodded from behind the bar as she walked up. Even though she was one of their long-time managers, she regularly filled in to give her bartenders a break.

Olivia secretly thought she liked the attention being behind the bar brought her. The redhead had to know she was a knockout.

"Hey, Red. Can I have a gin and tonic?"

Regina raised her eyebrows. "Hitting it hard tonight, huh?"

She laughed. The bartender was used to making her girly drinks or giving her the virgin type of cocktail. But tonight, Olivia needed something a little stronger. She didn't mind grabbing a cab to get home.

"It's been that kind of week."

She watched as Regina mixed the drink and pushed it across the bar toward her.

"Let me get whatever she's having," a voice declared over her shoulder.

Olivia turned and then smiled genuinely at her partner, Serena. The pretty brunette was always so bubbly. Even though she was an accountant, she'd had the idea to bring a Strippers for Beginners series of classes to the club that was really fun.

"It's good to see you out! You've been scarce lately." Serena gave her a quick, one-armed hug.

"Yeah, I've been busy."

"What?"

She had to repeat herself twice before Serena heard her over the music pulsing through the speakers.

"Your friend Georgie came to observe one of the cardio striptease classes. She's a sweetie."

Just like that Olivia was slammed back into *Mr. Totally Wrong for Her* territory. She'd just wanted to get a drink and forget about him but it seemed like no matter where she went, he found a way to follow her. Her apartment, her work, her bed, her dreams. Nowhere was safe. Worse, in the past few weeks she'd come to rely on his steady presence. For the first time in years, she'd felt like she had someone to lean on. It hurt almost more than her pride to lose that.

"Oh, Serena everything is so messed up. I fell for a member and I really thought we had something. I haven't had a boyfriend in so long but there was something so different about King. Even though I know he doesn't respect me at all, I still can't stop thinking about him. What do I do?"

Serena leaned closer and yelled over the music. "What did you say?"

She sighed. Was this really what she'd been reduced to? Serena was really nice and would have no problem giving her a shoulder to cry on if she needed one but she didn't know her that well. Had she really been reduced to dumping her problems on whoever happened to be sitting close by? This wasn't the place to have a deep conversation anyway. People didn't come to The Martini Room for deep thoughts. They came to forget their troubles.

Olivia plastered on a fake smile and raised her drink in Serena's direction. "Nothing worth repeating."

Serena laughed at something Regina said and Olivia wished this was a day that Elle was scheduled to visit the club. Her friend was a silent partner for a reason and due to her father's political career no one else at the club even knew her by her real name. They all knew her as Tess.

Whatever name she chose to go under, Olivia could have used a friend just then. Sure, she could always call her but this wasn't the kind of thing she wanted to explain over the phone.

This was the kind of problem that required an in-person girl power bitch session. But over the years as she'd worked single-mindedly toward her goal of financial independence, everything else in her life had taken a backseat, including friendships. The people she saw the most these days were her partners, her employees and... King.

As Olivia sipped her drink, she watched the people gyrating on the dance floor and felt how truly alone she really was.

Chapter 15

----

*K*ing had learned long ago that the best time to attack wasn't when your opponent was expecting it. So he waited a few days before he went to see Georgie.

It wasn't like he didn't have plenty to keep him busy. Reviewing the financials for the last quarter, handling a crisis with one of their top-tier investors and basically catching up on all the work he'd been ignoring the last few weeks while he'd been so mentally absent.

At the thought of Olivia, his hands tensed on the steering wheel. He parked in the drive in front of Kingsley Manor and got out. He'd called ahead so Jenner opened the door before he even hit the steps.

"Your father's waiting for you in his office, sir."

He nodded to the older man and watched as he ambled back toward the kitchen. The elderly woman who'd been in residence while he was growing up had retired not long after he entered college and moved to live closer to her grandchildren. Jenner had been hired after he was already an adult so they had a more distant relationship.

It had never bothered him until recently that he knew so little about someone who lived on his parents' property. But now, it seemed wrong that he'd never thought about it. He didn't know any of the maids' names either. Olivia would have said he was being a typical elitist. His lips twitched at the thought.

Then his heart clenched as it hit him anew that it didn't matter what Olivia thought now.

His father's office was on the main level in the East wing of the house. Thane looked up when he entered the room.

"King. I was surprised when you called."

He stood and came from behind the desk, motioning to the leather club chairs in the middle of the room.

"Have a seat. Tell me what's going on. Does this have anything to do with how Georgie's been moping around these past few days?"

They sat and King waved his hand to decline when his father asked if he wanted a drink.

"I'm here to check on her. I think she might have just partied a little too hard or something."

He'd debated how much to tell his parents. If he was a father he wouldn't appreciate being kept in the dark about what was going on but these types of situations were best if contained. The less people who knew the better.

Plus, there were some things a man didn't need to know about his daughter. As her older brother he was already permanently traumatized by the idea of her having sex. He didn't need to share that pain with his father.

His father sighed. The lines around his face were more pronounced and he looked tired. King realized he was looking at his own face in thirty years.

"That much was evident. She was brought home by James and appeared to have been drinking heavily. I'm not sure what's going on with that girl. I'm starting to think that encouraging her to marry Alex was the wrong move.

Things were different back in our day. You got married to someone your parents approved of and you had kids of your own. You tried not to fuck them up too badly. But the more time passes, the less confidence I have in the job your mother and I did. You kids don't seem to be adjusting to life on your own too well."

Shocked, King leaned back in his chair. "Dad, you don't mean that."

"I do. Colin barely has the motivation to get out of bed each day. Your sister seems to have no backbone and just wants to please everyone. Then there's you. I worry about you most."

"Why would you worry about me more than the others? I'm the only one who has a job! I've worked every day of my life to prove myself to you and it's never enough."

"Exactly. You work every day of your life and seem to live for that and nothing else. Colin is unmotivated but that can be fixed when he finds something that excites him. Your sister is a pleaser but eventually she'll find herself and decide what she wants to stand for. But you, I don't know how to help someone who doesn't want to care about anything."

The anger that had risen so quickly drained out of King just as fast. Everything his father had said reflected what he'd come to feel as well. He worked hard every day but it no longer brought him any joy. His joy had been the time he'd spent with Olivia learning how not to take himself so seriously.

"Maybe you're right."

His father looked surprised by the admission but he put a steadying hand on King's shoulder. "If you need to talk, I hope you know I'm here."

"I do. Thanks, Dad. I'm going to go check on Georgie."

His father didn't press him. "Good. I've always been glad you two are so close. So *you* can tell her that vase she knocked over when she stumbled in was a Ming. Your mother was pissed."

As King left the office his dad was still chuckling.

His sister had moved to a different room after she returned from college, one of the guest suites in the opposite wing from where his parents were. He knocked lightly on her door and as soon as it opened, stuck his foot in the crack so she couldn't slam it once she realized it was him.

Growing up with her gave him an advantage. He already knew all her defensive maneuvers.

"Go away, King. I really don't want to talk to you."

"When has that ever worked with me?"

Georgie rolled her eyes and then stepped aside. She closed the door behind him and then walked back to the couch in the middle of the sitting room. A cup of coffee and a magazine were on the table before her. He could hear the blare of the television coming from the direction of her bedroom.

"Are you okay?"

She sat back down and took a leisurely sip of her coffee.

"Oh no, I'm not okay. Just the idea of sex was too much for my feeble brain to handle. Surely I need a fainting couch to recover from the shock!"

King ignored her caustic tone. "This is serious, Georgie. What if someone had seen you? That isn't the kind of place for someone like you, kid. People are doing things that–"

"People are doing things that are completely consensual and having a great time while doing it. Maybe I wanted to find out what that was about before I get married. Or maybe I was scouting locations for my bachelorette party. It doesn't really matter why I was there, King. Because either way it's no one's damned business!"

King sat on the couch next to her and regarded his sister with new eyes. Completely uncowed by the situation, she seemed more upset about the invasion of her privacy than by anything she'd seen at Club VIP.

"I'm not sure what to say. You're right. Maybe it's time I realize my baby sister isn't a baby anymore. But that doesn't mean I like the way this went down. And I really don't like James seeing you like that."

"You're not the only one. God that guy needs to remove the stick from his ass. Or maybe that's why he was at Club VIP. Maybe he likes having something in his ass. I'm not judging."

King choked back a laugh, completely taken off guard by this side of his sister. "*Christ*, Georgie."

She shrugged. "What? He dragged me out of there like he had some right. He isn't my daddy or my boyfriend so who the hell does he think he is?"

"Well, whatever the case I'm glad he did. I still can't believe Olivia took you there without telling me."

Georgie slowly lowered her cup. "Oh no. Tell me you didn't screw things up with Olivia."

"Screw things up? She brought you to a sex club, Georgie! That is so far out of bounds I don't even know where the lines are anymore. Girls have tried to buddy up to you before to get on my good side. You know I hate that. It's so manipulative."

Georgie smacked her forehead with her hand.

"I can't even believe you sometimes, King. Olivia didn't buddy up to me. *I went to her.* I asked her to help me with a very sensitive thing and she did it, even though she really didn't want to."

"What are you talking about?"

She suddenly couldn't look at him and her cheeks turned bright red. "Something personal."

"This is going to make me want to throw up, isn't it?"

"Real mature. Look, you don't need to know the details but I wanted to go to Club VIP and if Olivia hadn't helped me, I would have just gone somewhere else. I think she wanted me where she could make sure I was safe."

He stood, his mind awash with the memories of his last moments with Olivia. She had looked so hurt, and suddenly he felt her pain as if it was his own. The things he'd said... How the hell could he ever make up for the things he'd said?

After hearing her story and observing how hard she'd worked to stand on her own two feet he'd blasted her as being "just a stripper" and called her club "trashy".

She'd never said a word in her own defense even though she could have easily thrown Georgie under the bus. Instead she'd kept his sister's secret, even when it would have been to her benefit to tell him the whole story.

In short, she'd been the same big-hearted, loving Olivia and he'd been the same arrogant, bad-tempered King.

"How do I fix this?" he asked without preamble.

Georgie didn't look too hopeful. "You might not be able to fix this. Women are like glass. Strong on the surface but easily shattered."

"That doesn't make me feel better."

"It wasn't meant to. If you want her, then you'd better be prepared to do the work. She's worth it, King. She could have easily tattled on me to get on your good side but she didn't. Olivia is the real deal." She stood and kissed him on the cheek. "Good luck, big brother. You're a jerk sometimes but your heart is in the right place."

"Thanks, I think."

"Oh and by the way. Tell James I owe him a nut punch."

King was laughing by the time he left but his mind was already formulating a plan. He'd hurt Olivia and he could only hope she would give him a chance to show her how sorry he was.

———————————

Chapter 16

———————————

Olivia watched as her best friend stammered through a greeting with the head of the Mentor Science program. As promised, she'd been by his side all night and helped to carry conversations when Bennett got awkward. Surprisingly, it hadn't happened as often as she'd expected.

Her best friend was a changed man.

She observed him with new eyes. He was handsome in a perfectly fitted taupe suit that brought out the green in his hazel eyes. Bennett came from a multi-racial family just like she did and tanned heavily in the summers. His pale skin was burnished a darker golden tone than she was used to and his usually unruly curly hair was tamed with... was that gel? Bennett was using hair product now?

Her best friend was pretty hot.

It was so weird to see him like this and under different circumstances it would have made Olivia happy. For years she'd thought that she and Bennett would make a good match except for their lack of sexual chemistry so it should have been a pleasant shock that her bestie had a different side to him. There was just one problem.

She was miserable.

You don't owe him anything. She repeated it over and over inside her head, hoping it would eventually sink in. It felt like she was betraying King. Her heart hadn't accepted that he wasn't hers anymore and truthfully, never had been.

Clearly she'd been fooling herself the entire time.

"Are you okay, Boo?"

Olivia glanced at Bennett who watched her with perceptive eyes. Even though she'd been smiling and laughing all night, he'd picked up on her subdued mood. She shook her head. This was their night. They hadn't had as much time to visit each other over the past year and she'd missed him. She wasn't going to let thoughts of King ruin her chance to catch up with the one man who'd never let her down.

"I'm going to be fine. Tell me about what's new with your family. I haven't seen everyone since Nick's wedding."

Over the next hour, he showed her pictures of his adorable nephews and his newest niece, who Olivia still hadn't met. She even managed to get Bennett on the dance floor. His oldest brother was a well-known music producer so he'd shown her the new dances that he'd learned from watching one of Jackson's music videos.

Olivia had never laughed so hard in her life watching her brainy best friend attempt to do something he called "The Dot".

She was quite sure he'd gotten the name wrong but it didn't even matter. He was willing to humiliate himself to make her smile and by the time she caught her breath, she made a decision. There was never going to be another man who loved her more than Bennett Alexander.

It was time to stop thinking about the man who'd hurt her and focus on the man who'd done nothing but love her.

"Let's take a walk. It's nice outside this evening."

Bennett looked confused but accepted the hand she held out. "Sure. The Director mentioned that the gardens in this hotel are exceptional. I'd love to see what kind of plants they used."

They crossed the ballroom and emerged through a set of double doors onto a stone walkway. Olivia gasped. The gardens had been styled into a maze, the hedges trimmed to form short walls. Lights sparkled in the bushes giving it a magical feeling.

"This is beautiful."

Bennett walked up to the bush and peered at the leaves. "Interesting. I was expecting Boxwoods but it appears they've gone with American Arborvitae."

Olivia grasped his hand. If she didn't rein him in he might end up on the ground to see what the soil felt like or something.

"Bennett. I wanted to say thank you for bringing me with you tonight. This has been a lot of fun. I've missed just hanging out with you."

"I've missed hanging out with you, too." He pushed his glasses up absently. That had always been one of his nervous tells.

He was such a sweetheart, that he'd be nervous around her after everything they'd been through. He'd seen her at her very worst, after all. But that was Bennett.

At that moment, she decided to just go for it. She'd never know for sure if they could have worked out unless she made a move. He wasn't going to do it. It wasn't Bennett's style to be aggressive. So just like when they were young, she would do it for him.

She grabbed him by the lapels and kissed him.

Olivia closed her eyes and stood on her toes since he was so much taller. His lips were soft and his shoulders were broader than she'd thought as she stretched her arms around his neck. But even though he was tall and handsome and loved her, it wasn't enough. He wasn't the one she imagined when she closed her eyes.

He wasn't King.

Finally Olivia realized that Bennett was as rigid as a statue. Not only was he not kissing her back but he might not have even been breathing.

"Bennett? Take a breath."

He gasped audibly and his arms came up to hold hers.

She bit her lip. "You didn't feel anything either, did you?"

He suddenly looked relieved. Olivia would have laughed if he hadn't looked so genuinely distressed.

"No, I didn't. I'm sorry. I would never want to hurt your feelings, Boo."

"You didn't. I'm in love with someone else. But I wanted it to be you. Stupid, huh?"

"No, it's not stupid. You're one of the smartest people I know."

"There's no way that's true. You're surrounded by literal geniuses all the time."

"Understanding science isn't the only way to be intelligent. For years, you've been the one person I could count on to accept me as I am. You're that person for a lot of people, Livvy. Somehow you know how to be a great friend to everyone in your life. Which seems pretty smart to me."

Suddenly she was overcome with affection for him. Over the years, through thick and thin, he'd been there. Despite having issues with her father, Olivia had never thought all men were bad. How could she when she had one of the best men out there in her corner?

"God, I love you so much, you know that?"

"I love you, too. I always will." Bennett squeezed her arms again and then kissed her on the forehead.

They stayed just like that for a little while and Olivia tried not to cry when she understood what he was really saying. Suddenly his relief made total sense. Bennett was in love with someone else, too. No matter how much he loved her, someone else was his top priority now.

Which was as it should be.

"Go. I can take a cab home."

She could see that he was reluctant to leave her but just because she'd had the bad taste to fall for the wrong guy, didn't mean she wanted Bennett to ruin a good thing. If he'd found someone who understood him, she wanted that for him. He deserved love.

"I'll be fine. And someday soon, I want to meet her."

He blushed. "I just hope she hasn't changed her mind about me."

She watched him leave and then took a seat on one of the benches, watching the lights twinkle on the hedges.

"Goodbye my friend," she whispered.

King had officially hit stalker status.

It had taken him a few days to get up his nerve to talk to Olivia and once he'd finally decided on the appropriate level of groveling, he'd parked outside of her place only to see her come outside and greet *that guy*.

He scowled as he glanced across the room to where Olivia was dancing with him. He was a nerdy-looking guy who danced like he had no concept of rhythm. It hadn't even been a week and she'd already replaced him? Not that he could really blame her. Of course after dealing with him she'd probably wanted a guy who was actually *nice*.

But seriously, did she think a guy who looked like the human equivalent of skim milk could satisfy her?

Unaware of his torment, Olivia threw her head back and laughed, completely at ease with his glasses-wearing rival.

Skim milk could make her laugh, apparently. *Damn it.*

When they walked through the doors leading outside, King followed at a discreet distance. He couldn't just barge out there. After the way he'd spoken to Olivia he wouldn't be surprised if she never wanted to talk to him again. He needed to approach her carefully.

Then someone else opened the doors and his heart dropped. Olivia had her arms around the guy's neck and was kissing him passionately.

He closed his eyes. It looked like she was fully committed to moving on from him. He walked to the bar and ordered a drink. His plan was going to require some adjustments.

As crazy as it made him to see Olivia wrapped around some other guy, he wasn't giving up. He'd never been as lost as he'd been this past week. They hadn't been together long but he didn't need more time to see the obvious.

She made his life better. She made *him* better.

He was an asshole and he'd messed up. But he was hoping she'd felt something for him, too. If there was any chance she was willing to forgive him, he had to try.

He paused with his drink in his hand when he saw nerd boy come in.

Alone.

Where the hell was Olivia?

He watched as the guy left the ballroom. Maybe he was pulling up the car. This might be his only chance to talk to Olivia alone.

He stuffed a twenty in the tip jar for the bartender and rose. From the signs in the entryway, this was some kind of award ceremony but he couldn't figure out what industry it was for. Most of the attendees seemed like the serious type so he wondered if it was some sort of academic function.

When he stepped outside, Olivia looked up. She was sitting on a bench right in front of the doors.

She laughed bitterly. "Of course you're here. What do you want? Another chance to slum it with a dirty stripper?"

Although her tone was angry, King didn't miss the genuine hurt in her voice.

"I don't know what you heard..."

"Yes, you do. You know *exactly* what I heard."

Caught, King told himself it was time to lay it all out there. Because she was right. If he was going to apologize, it couldn't be a half-hearted effort. He had to own all his shit and put the blame where it belonged. Squarely on his shoulders.

"You're right. I know exactly what you heard. Me and my equally idiotic best friend talking about you like another business deal."

She crossed her arms. "Well, at least you admit it."

"I do. That's exactly how I've always thought of relationships. Something that I had to accomplish to make my parents happy. Or to piss them off. Or to keep control of the family empire. That's what happened that night at Club VIP. My father had forced me into a corner and I thought, you know what, I'll really stick it to the old man. I'll bring home someone that'll shame and embarrass them. I'll make them sorry they ever tried to marry me off. But then something insane happened."

He sat on the bench next to her. She scooted over so their legs wouldn't touch.

"The girl I brought home to embarrass them, charmed them. The girl I was stupid enough to think was beneath me, taught me what it meant to be happy."

She swiped at her face but still wouldn't look at him. He realized in that moment just how deeply he'd hurt her.

"Everything I thought I was so sure about turned out to be completely false. And in the midst of all of that, I fell in love with you."

Olivia scoffed.

"You don't get to say that to me. This is not love. You don't talk about someone you love like that. I told you things I've never told anyone. And you were judging me the whole time."

A curl had escaped from her low bun and his fingers itched to push it back behind her ear. It felt like it had been years since he'd touched her. He wished he could go back and do so many things differently but he'd especially cherish those last moments before he'd shattered the trust between them.

You never think your last moments with someone will the last ones you have.

"You're right. This is not how you treat someone you love. You don't treat her badly and then think *I'm sorry* is enough. Then you don't follow her like a stalker and watch while she's kissing another man."

Olivia didn't even smile.

"I want you to go, King. If you care about me like you say you do, then you'll give me some time. I'm not sure I can forget the things you said so easily."

He stood, wishing there was something else he could say. But in the end, all he could do was respect her wishes. His biggest mistake before had been reacting out of anger and not trusting her.

If they were ever going to have a chance, he had to be willing to do what Georgie had said. *Put in the work.*

"I'm going to leave because it's what you want. But that doesn't mean I'm giving up."

As he walked away, he thought he heard her whisper, "*I hope you don't.*"

Chapter 17

For the next week, Olivia took the vacation days she'd been saving up. It had been over a year since she'd taken off more than a few days at a time. It was strange not to go to the club everyday and not as relaxing as she'd thought it would be.

Without work to distract her, it gave her nothing but time to reflect on just how empty her life was.

The anger had numbed her at first. She'd been so awash in hurt and pain thinking about the things King had said that she hadn't had a chance to reflect on the hole he'd left in her life. But now that the shock and anger had faded with a little time, it was evident in the little things.

Whenever she saw something weird she wanted to call and tell him about it. When she had a great idea for the Club, he was the one she wanted to share it with. When she was sad or missed her mother, his arms were the ones she wanted to hold her.

Over the past month she'd gotten used to him being there as her sounding board, confidante and comfort.

She missed him. How stupid was that? He was the only man who'd ever torn her heart out and she missed him.

The doorbell rang and Olivia stood. She'd been in the house for four days straight and was starting to forget what fresh air felt like. This wasn't healthy. She'd asked for space from King and he'd respected that but now she was starting to wish he hadn't suddenly decided to listen.

When she opened the door, she jumped back at the explosion of flowers before her. A kaleidoscope of colors, the bouquet was so huge she couldn't even see the guy holding them. That was probably a good thing since she was only wearing a long t-shirt and her hair was up in a ratty bun.

"Delivery for Miss Olivia Reyes?"

"Yes, that's me. Here I'll just take these." She managed to wrap her hands around the vase and then deposited it carefully on the entryway table.

The delivery man held out his clipboard so she could sign. After he left, she searched through the huge bouquet looking for a card, strangely let down when she didn't find one. Not that there was any doubt who they were from. She shook her head.

Only King would send her such a ridiculous bouquet. He never did anything in half-measures.

Even hurting her. He'd hit right at the heart of her deepest insecurities and it had torn her up.

The doorbell rang again. When she opened it, King looked up. He was wearing his usual suit but for some reason, he held a pair of boxing gloves.

"May I come in?"

She stepped back so he could come inside. He smiled when he saw the huge bouquet. Then he turned to her and held out the gloves.

"These are for you."

Confused, Olivia accepted them. "Boxing gloves?"

"Yeah. I hit below the belt and now you can, too. Go ahead. Take your best shot. Georgie told me both James and I deserve a nut punch for how we've behaved."

It was so ridiculous, *so King,* that Olivia was startled into laughing.

"Well, at least you're laughing this time. I'd rather see that than tears. I never want to see that again." He ran his hands over his hair.

For the first time Olivia took a close look at him. The bags under his eyes were darker and more pronounced and he sported what looked like three days worth of stubble on his face. She'd never seen him like this.

"You look like shit," she whispered.

"That's better than how I feel. I hurt the only woman I've ever cared about."

"You did. Hurt me, I mean." She put the boxing gloves down on the table next to the flowers. "But I realized something this past week."

"What did you realize, baby?"

Her heart fluttered a little at the endearment.

"For a long time, I never cared what anyone thought of me. I did what I needed to do and I didn't look back. After years of trying to gain my father's approval, I realized his love came with conditions. He believes in sin but not forgiveness. So I stopped trying and relied only on myself. I built everything I have on my own."

"And you should be proud of that. I had no right to talk about you or the club that way. I was such an idiot."

"Yeah, you were. But I realized the only reason it hurt so much is because I care about what you think of me. I care about you."

He pulled her into his arms and she finally stopped resisting. He held her face between his hands gently and kissed all over her face.

"I'm so sorry, Olivia. Forgive me. I'm not so good at this love thing. It's never happened before."

She bit her lip. "You love me? When you said it before I didn't want to believe it."

"I. Love. You." Each word was punctuated by a kiss and every single kiss punched straight through to her heart.

"I love you too, King. Even when I don't like you very much."

He cut off her words with a kiss on her mouth and suddenly their hands were everywhere, frantically caressing and yanking at their clothes. *Yes*, Olivia thought. She wanted him all over her. Wanted to be as close to him as she could physically get. They walked backward, their mouths still connected until they landed on the couch.

"Hurry," she whispered and he moaned against her lips.

He felt it too, this urgency to seal their emotional connection with a physical one. She loved him and he loved her. All the hurt, the pain and the apologies seemed not to matter now that they were together again. He'd hurt her but forgiveness was something she was intimately acquainted with since she'd worked so hard to gain it herself.

He pushed his pants down and her t-shirt up. When he thrust into her, her head fell back and she closed her eyes, savoring having him back where he belonged. He rested his forehead against hers, not moving, just breathing with her.

"Don't leave me again, angel. Scream at me, hurt me, *hell*, give me a nut punch if you need to. But don't leave. I need you too much for that."

"I need you, too."

He started to move then and she wrapped her legs around his back. Everything faded away and all that was left was the two of them. She arched under him, the physical sensations suddenly too sharp.

After living without him, she was overwhelmed by how *much* he was. He was it for her and all the feelings she'd tried to hold back for the past week rushed her full force. She clung to his shoulders as all of the emotions, the pain and the love coalesced into a storm of pleasure that dragged her into a shattering release.

King clenched her so tightly, like he was scared she'd escape if he didn't hold on tightly enough. He leaned up slightly and kept his eyes on hers so she got to see it when he lost himself. On his face she saw nothing but naked desire and all-consuming love.

Afterward, he lifted her and sat on the couch with her in his lap. She cuddled up against him, enjoying being in his arms again. He shifted slightly and tipped up her chin so he could see her face.

"I meant what I said. I love you. And I'm going to make sure you never have a reason to doubt that. I'm not a good person, Liv, but you make me want to be better. Every day. I'm the one who isn't worthy of you."

Her heart swelled and she buried her face in his shoulder. Although she'd believed him when he'd apologized, it meant even more that he wanted to make sure not to ever hurt her like that again.

"You're not a bad person. You're just a bad boy type. My bad King."

"Maybe one day you'll be my bad Queen and keep me in line."

She jerked back so fast she almost fell off his lap. "Don't even joke about that."

"Who's joking?"

Olivia punched him in the shoulder. "Ow. Where are my boxing gloves?"

King kissed her again. "It's okay, I'll convince you eventually. I always get what I want remember?"

"Stop." She put a finger over his lips but secretly Olivia was looking forward to finding out what a future with her bad boy would look like.

He lifted her in his arms. "Convincing you could take awhile. Maybe I should get started now."

———————————————

Chapter 18

———————————————

Not too far in the future...

*I*f anyone had ever told King that he'd be one of those pathetic men who couldn't even go one night without his girlfriend, he would have laughed in their face. In fact he would've wagered half his net worth that it would never happen.

He'd be quite a few million lighter in the wallet by now if that had been the case. It had only been a few minutes since he'd left Olivia in the car and he was already wondering what she was doing or if she needed anything.

Pathetic.

But also exactly why he was standing in the lobby of a rustic mountain cabin.

"So everything is set for tonight?" King glanced over his shoulder to be sure Olivia hadn't followed him inside.

He'd told her to relax in the car while he got them checked in. Pulling her away from the club in the midst of December had been a hard sell but she'd eventually agreed they both could use a weekend getaway. The remote cabin resort in the mountains of Virginia was perfect.

"Yes sir, Mr. Kingsley." Mrs. English, the cheerful proprietor of The Olde English B&B, had been his primary contact setting up this important weekend.

"Good. Because we almost got in an accident on the way here and then we had a flat tire. I'm starting to feel like the universe is conspiring against me."

Although he couldn't understand why. The universe should know better than anyone that he needed Olivia like he needed air.

The past few months had only proven what he'd known since the moment he'd thought he lost her. She was his reason for getting up each day and his comfort when he went to sleep each night.

Not only did she make him happy but she fit right in with his family like she'd always been there. She smoothed the rough edges of his relationship with Colin and kept Georgina from blistering his ear with TMI details that he did NOT want to know.

He didn't even want to think about what he'd interrupted in his sister's room a few weeks ago.

Ugh.

He was still trying to bleach his brain of images that could scar him for life.

But through it all, Olivia had been there. She made life better. She made him better. Obviously she was way too good for him.

He was selfish enough to ask her to marry him anyway.

"There's no need to worry. Your dinner tonight will be spectacular."

"It's dessert that I'm worried about."

Mrs. English smiled. "Her tiramisu will be perfect."

King immediately felt his blood pressure start to rise. "Chocolate mousse. The tiramisu is mine."

"Of course. I misspoke. The chocolate mousse will be perfect."

King tugged at the collar that was suddenly strangling him. "Maybe we should—"

Mrs. English cleared her throat suddenly and tilted her head to the left, his only warning before Olivia appeared at his side.

"Hey! I decided to get out and stretch my legs." She nodded hello to Mrs. English.

"Hey, baby. Perfect timing. Our room is ready now."

With a meaningful glance at Mrs. English, he picked up the ancient-looking key she'd placed on the counter and offered his arm to Olivia.

Before the day was done, she'd be the future Mrs. Kingsley.

———

*K*ing figured he'd been crappy company since he was so nervous about their special dinner that night. Olivia hadn't seemed to notice though, completely charmed by every aspect of their mountain cabin getaway.

She'd cajoled him into taking a short hike around the property even though it was damn near freezing. Then she'd insisted on sitting downstairs in the quaint sitting room to enjoy the fire. Now it was finally time for dinner and he was starting to get worried that he wouldn't be able to get her out of the room.

"Aren't you hungry?"

Olivia rolled over and buried her face in the pillows. "Not really."

"Because I'm starving. You know, after all that hiking."

"I'm sleepy." She curled up and put her hands beneath her cheek the way she always did right before she fell asleep for the night. Oh god. He knew that look. It was her comfy, my-bra-is-off, sleeping position. Which meant that if he didn't figure out how to get her down to the dining room his plan was ruined.

"Chocolate!" He yelled, desperate.

Her eyes popped open. "What is going on with you?"

"Nothing. I just heard they have a really good chocolate mousse here."

She sat up looking completely alert. "Really? That's worth getting up for!"

King let out a sigh of relief. He hadn't thought the hardest part of proposing would be getting her to leave the room.

An hour later they were seated in the small dining room finishing up a delicious steak dinner. He'd snuck off ten minutes ago to meet Mrs. English in the kitchen. She'd promised to make sure the custom engagement ring he'd had designed for Olivia was placed right on top of her chocolate mousse.

It was only a few minutes after the waiter had cleared their dinner dishes that another waiter arrived with their desserts.

"*Ooh look at this*. My mouth is watering." Olivia dug out a huge bite with her spoon and hummed in delight at the first taste.

King took an absentminded bite of his own. The top of her chocolate mousse had so much whipped cream that he couldn't tell where they'd placed the ring. What if they'd lost it? Or mixed up the orders and someone's ninety-nine year old grandma was about to get a five-carat ring stuck in her dentures?

Just when he was about to hit full-on panic mode, Olivia's eyes lit up.

"Oh my gosh. King, this is amazing."

He smiled. She must have found it. Just then he swallowed and his throat closed. He coughed.

Then coughed again.

"King?"

Just as she stood up, he coughed again and the ring landed in his lap. He closed his hand around it before Olivia could see it. He glanced behind him to the waiter who looked ashen.

The waiter mouthed *"Sorry"* before turning around and scampering into the kitchen.

So much for the perfect proposal.

King sighed. He'd do it tomorrow and plan it all himself. This was too important to risk getting wrong.

Olivia caressed his hair. "Let's go relax in our room."

"I'm sorry you didn't get to eat your dessert."

She kissed his cheek. "We can come back tomorrow."

King followed her out, the ring still clutched in his palm. Considering how the weekend was starting out, he was almost scared to find out what was in store for the next day.

Universe: 3

King: 0

———

Olivia smothered a grin as she moved around the room, pretending she didn't notice King melting down right behind her. Counting on her fingers, she went through her list of campfire s'mores essentials one more time.

Basket. *Check.*

Blanket. *Check.*

Wine. *Check.*

Portable speaker. *Check.*

Did she actually need to check it all again?

Not really.

But was it crazy amusing to watch King losing his patience?

Absolutely.

She finally decided to give him a break. He would bite a hole through his lip if she didn't take pity on him soon.

"Seriously, babe. You have to relax. We're on vacation. I can't wait to make s'mores and look at the stars."

King sighed. "I know. I'm relaxed. I am."

Her eyes dropped to where his fist was clenched around the end of the blanket she'd asked him to place in their basket. Then she shook her head.

"Right. Relaxed. You totally look it."

That made him laugh.

"Okay, I'm *trying* to relax. Rome wasn't built in a day."

He pulled her into his arms. His nose settled against the side of her neck the way it always did sending a little shiver down her spine.

It was something Liv didn't think she'd ever really get used to, the casual way he made her feel completely essential to him. She loved the soft, contented sound he always made when he pulled her into his arms that could banish even the worst of days.

King wasn't a naturally demonstrative man, much more likely to grunt instead of explaining his feelings. That was what made all the little things he did to show his feelings matter so much. Olivia cherished every single one.

Things such as planning a spur of the moment long weekend at a romantic B&B.

"I'm not sure why you're so on edge. This has been the perfect weekend already. We slept late and lolled around in bed all morning like two lazy slugs. Then we had that amazing brunch."

He bit her neck, making her jump. "Not sure I like our morning in bed being given the same weight as French toast."

She laughed. "I definitely enjoyed taking a bite out of you more than the French toast."

"That's what I'm talking about." He glanced at his watch and then grabbed the picnic basket. "Okay, time to go!"

Olivia hustled to keep up, stopping briefly to grab her coat. By the time she caught up with King he was already outside marching toward the firepit the proprietor of the bed and breakfast had promised was perfect for making s'mores.

"What is the hurry? King, we're on vacation. It's not like we have reservations."

He slowed. Barely. "I know. I just want to be sure we get a good spot. You never know."

Olivia looked around incredulously. The bed and breakfast was located in a tiny town in Virginia called Broken River. From what she'd seen the prior evening on arrival there wasn't much here other than the B&B itself, a general store and a lot of farmland.

"I think we're okay if we take our time."

She fell into step next to him and watched his profile. King was always so confident that it was unsettling to see him like this. Even in a situation where he had no idea what was going on, he was a master at keeping his emotions hidden.

When they reached the firepit, he placed the basket next to one of the wooden chairs. Olivia took a seat and then pulled the blanket out of the basket while King tended to the fire. It was cold but they'd dressed for the weather and she found the brisk air refreshing. She took a deep breath, enjoying the luxury of having nowhere she needed to be.

"It's beautiful here. So quiet."

King smiled and for the first time that day, it looked genuine. "This is exactly what we both needed."

Olivia pushed a marshmallow through one of the skewers provided while King uncorked the wine. The B&B had even provided mini-wineglasses inside the basket. The perfect romance kit.

She sat forward to hold her marshmallow over the flames before making another for King. They sat in companionable silence for a few minutes before King glanced over at her.

"Could you ever see yourself living somewhere like this? In the future, I mean."

Olivia shrugged. "You're forgetting I was raised somewhere similar. New Haven isn't this tiny but it's green and beautiful just like this. When I was a little girl, all I knew was our land. It seemed to go on as far as the eye could see. We used to sit outside on clear nights just like this and wish on the stars."

"What did you wish for?"

The serious tone of his voice alerted her that this wasn't just a random question. His blue eyes were so intense she sat up slightly, almost dropping her marshmallow.

"Is everything okay?"

He took a deep breath. "Everything is better than it's ever been before. The past year with you has shown me what it's like to actually live. Each day I keep expecting it to wear off."

"For what to wear off?" she whispered.

He took her hand. "Whatever spell you cast on me that's made me need you so much."

Suddenly she couldn't breathe. "Clearly I'm very devious."

He laughed. "You are. Now that you're in my life, I hate every moment that I don't get to spend with you. All the things that used to mean so much to me are suddenly completely empty. Since that's entirely your fault, I'm hoping you'll take pity on me and supply the cure."

"What's the cure?"

He held out his skewer in her direction. Liv looked at it in confusion. "The cure is a marshmallow?"

"No, it's ..."

He jumped up suddenly and Olivia watched as he started turning in circles. Then he dropped to his knees and started looking at the ground. Puzzled, she leaned forward trying to see what he was doing.

"Damn it all to hell!"

Startled, Olivia fell over when she leaned too far. "King, what is going on?"

"It fell off! It was only on there for a second!" He let out a frustrated yell and then put both his middle fingers up to the sky.

Unsure of what to make of his behavior, Olivia covered her mouth to keep from laughing. "That's okay. I understand. We can make you another."

"Even the marshmallows are conspiring against me!"

At this point she couldn't hold back her laughter anymore. "Babe, it's fine."

His hands tore through his hair until the strands were standing straight up. "It wasn't the marshmallow. It was... oh for fucks sake."

He walked next to her and dropped down on one knee. Her laughter faded as he took her hand.

"I was trying so hard to make it special. I wanted you to have the big ring on the dessert moment because you deserve that, Liv. You deserve magic and moonlight and everything I have to give. But I can't wait another second to ask if you'll be my wife. It's been hard enough to wait this long because I feel like I'm dying every second that I don't know your answer."

Olivia couldn't even speak with the huge lump in her throat so she just nodded. If she hadn't already loved him madly, the dramatic look of relief on his face would have pushed her off that cliff.

How had she gone through life not knowing what it was like to be loved this way? To be wanted so badly that a man acted like her answer was all he was living for.

When she finally could breathe, she put a hand on his cheek. "Of course my answer is yes, you crazy man. What would I do without you in my life?"

King kissed her so long they were both panting for air by the time they broke apart. "Hell if I know but I don't want to find out."

"At least now I know why you've been acting so strangely since yesterday." She laughed remembering how weird he'd been last night at dinner. "Oh god, the dessert!"

"Yeah, the kitchen got it mixed up so instead of you getting a diamond ring, I almost had to get the Heimlich."

"My poor baby. You really have been through a lot planning this, huh?"

"The universe put me through my paces this weekend trying to ruin my perfect proposal but as long as I have you, I don't care."

Olivia grinned when she noticed a glint of something shiny in the dirt by his foot. She pointed and King turned to look.

"Maybe the universe is trying to make amends." He lifted the ring carefully and blew it off. Then he slid it on her finger.

"Holy hunk of carbon," Liv whispered. "You really were trying to make a statement."

He grinned. "Only the best for my queen."

"You know it, mister. Maybe you should take your future queen upstairs and worship me properly."

She shrieked as he lifted her suddenly, running for the cabin. Over his shoulder, she marveled at the beautiful display of stars on show, remembering that she'd never answered King's question earlier.

She'd have to be sure to tell him he'd already made her wish come true.

I hope you enjoyed BAD KING!

Ready to read about King's sister? Georgie's story, the RITA® Winner *Bad Blood* is available now! *When my best friend's little sister gets left at the altar, I'd do anything to help her. Until she asks for the one thing I can't give. One night. No rules.*

Bonus Material:
Everyone's favorite anti-social genius, Bennett Alexander, has been invited to a bachelor party. If you think Ben's awkward now, imagine how he'll react in a strip club. LOL :)>

To read it free, join the VIP list at minxmalone.com/news.

Also, if you've enjoyed this book, *please* consider **leaving a review**. Reviews are the best gift you can give an author!

NEXT: an excerpt of Bennett's book

Start reading now at minxmalone.com/justonething

Bennett Alexander is a bonafide genius. He runs his family's farming cooperative, speaks four languages and is about to apply for his tenth patent. But the one thing he never mastered is how to be cool. His childhood friend Olivia is the only one who "gets" him.

Katie Mason is in over her head. Taking care of her two kids and dealing with the aftermath of her divorce leaves her exhausted at the end of every day. By the time she realizes her ex-husband left her with a mountain of bills, she'll take any job available, including working for the strange, brilliant man who scrambles her brain whenever they meet.

When Bennett hires her, the task is simple: teach him to act normal so he can win the heart of his first love. But there's just one thing: Katie seems to like him exactly the way he is. Now he needs to figure out how to make teacher + student = 4ever.

EXCERPT of *Just One Thing*
© March 2017 M. Malone

Something was up.

Katie finished organizing the mail that had come in the prior day and wiped down the stainless steel table that Bennett had just finished working on. He hadn't asked her to assist this time and she thought it was really sweet that he was taking the effort to try not to give her anything that would scare her.

Then she frowned. It was sweet of him to try to protect her feelings but it was hardly going to help her prove her worth as an assistant. She really wanted to stretch her wings and get used to doing things outside of her comfort zone.

She'd always been the good girl, the one who followed the rules and tried to keep the peace. Not that there was anything wrong with that but it made for a pretty boring existence. Don had loved to throw that in her face, that she wasn't spontaneous. Well, no more. Things were different now and she would be different, too. She wanted to shake things up and make a difference in the world. Katie sighed.

Nothing she'd ever done would be considered revolutionary or exciting.

"Can I help with that?" she asked when Bennett appeared holding several glass beakers.

She'd never tell him this but whenever he asked her to fetch one or the other, it always made her giggle because some of the liquids looked like Kool-Aid.

"No, I've got it. You can leave early if you want."

Frustrated, Katie slapped her hand down on the stainless steel table between them. "What gives? I know you only hired me to get Ri off your back but I can do more than sort mail."

"That's not true," Bennett said finally, after blinking at her in surprise for several seconds. "I didn't just hire you because Ridley suggested it. That was the catalyst, yes but I hired you because I wanted to."

Katie gave him a disbelieving look. "So far all I've done is grab a few things for you, clean up a little and sort mail. You don't need an assistant for that."

"You've been very helpful," Bennett countered.

"I'm a disaster. Try again."

"Um, actually ... I must confess to an ulterior motive." His eyes wouldn't meet hers all of a sudden and then he turned bright red.

Oh boy. Katie was starting to have an idea where this was going. This whole deal had been too good to be true from the start. Bennett had told her himself that he wasn't socially adept so he probably couldn't see just how screwed up approaching a woman like this was. Not to mention that if he was blushing like that, he probably had some weird fetish that he was going to spring on her. He was a good-looking guy even if he was a little odd so the only way he'd need to pay for sex was if he wanted her to do something pretty strange.

"You look like you're about to be sick," Bennett observed after almost a full minute of awkward silence.

Katie struggled to get her facial expression under control. Even if she was completely offended that he'd thought to hire her as a way to hit on her, this was still Jackson's brother. The Alexanders had always been amazing to her and she didn't want things to be weird when they saw each other in the future.

Or *weirder*, anyway.

There was no way things wouldn't be awkward when she saw him and she wasn't sure how she'd explain things to Ridley who adored her brother-in-law.

"I think maybe you've got the wrong idea about me. I'm desperate for money but not that desperate that I'm up for anything weird."

Bennett's eyes rounded. His mouth opened and closed a few times before he finally managed to speak.

"Wait, you think I brought you here as a *sexual* overture? I have no idea what in my statements or behavior could have indicated *that.*"

Bennett looked truly perplexed. His confusion made it obvious that he hadn't been thinking anything of the sort which made Katie feel pretty stupid.

"Sorry. It's just when you said you had an ulterior motive, I assumed—"

"Actually this brings up a good point." Bennett interrupted. "I have no idea how the things I do or say are perceived by others. I make social missteps and cause offense quite regularly due to this. That's why I need you. To teach me."

"You want me to teach you how to be ... non-offensive?"

"*Normal.* I want you to teach me how to be *normal.*"

"Um, okay." Katie sat on the stool at the counter. Her eyes landed on the small plants growing under the clear domes. She looked around the room, taking in the string of chemical equations on the chalkboard across from them and the jars of strangely colored liquids in beakers on the next table. Suddenly she laughed.

"Actually that makes way more sense than, you know, the other thing."

Bennett smiled a little at that. "I saw you when you were disciplining your son that day. After dinner."

Katie nodded that she remembered. He'd asked her a lot of questions that evening, about whether she got frustrated correcting her children. It had definitely been a strange conversation.

"Well, it occurred to me then that mothers correct their children a little at a time. They're able to train them effectively because they're usually present to intervene when they behave inappropriately. That's exactly what I need."

"You need a mother? You already have a mother and she's amazing." Katie wasn't sure where he was going with this because Julia was practically the blueprint for the perfect mother.

"She is amazing. That's not what I mean. I need someone to watch my behavior and correct me in the moment when I misstep."

"Sorry but I have to wonder, wouldn't this have worked the first time when Julia was raising you?"

Katie crossed her fingers that he wouldn't take offense at the question. When he didn't say anything, she could have kicked herself. "Stupid question? Never mind."

"Don't ever be afraid to question things. That's the mark of a scientific mind," Bennett mumbled, sounding like he was only half-paying attention to the conversation. He stroked his chin a few times and then his lips moved silently.

Katie realized that he was talking to himself.

"Bennett, are you listening?"

"Hmm? Oh yes, I was just thinking about the fact that my mother's birthday is coming up."

When he noticed the look on her face, he shook his head hard. "See, this is what I mean! I drift off in conversation, go off on tangents and I need someone to bring me back to things. Anyway, where were we?"

"Wondering why you think this would work if it didn't stick the first go around when Julia was raising you?"

"My mother loves me too much to give me the harsh truth. She loves me as I am, even as strange as I am. She would never tell me something that she thought might hurt my feelings. But I need someone who can tell me the harsh truth."

"I don't want to hurt you either, Bennett. I like you."

Bennett gaped at her. "You do? Why?"

Katie laughed. "Um, you're brilliant and you're actually really funny sometimes. Maybe you just need to find more people who share your interests? Like, I don't know ... another scientist?"

Bennett gestured around them. "Look around. I want more than just this in my life. All I do is work and sleep and then wake up to work some more. But the only thing I know how to do is approach problems logically. Getting a tutor seems logical to me. I know this is unorthodox, but will you help me?"

Katie was pretty sure this entire thing had a high proba-
bility of being a terrible idea. But she discovered something
about herself in that moment. She had a really hard time
saying no to a handsome face and a sincere request.

"I'll help you. On one condition."

"What's that?" Bennett looked wary.

"You have to actually listen to what I have to say. If we're
going to do this, it's not going to be easy and you're probably going to hate the things I suggest but I have to know
you're serious about this."

He shrugged. "I dabble in genetic engineering of organic
compounds. If I can do that then I should be able to handle
this, right?"

Start reading now at minxmalone.com/justonething

FOR THE FIRST TIME EVER MY ROOSTER WON'T CROW.

I can't believe it either. It's a tragedy.

Years of perfect performance and now this traitor decides to get picky. And the only woman who makes little Milo stand up and *c-ck a doodle doo* is my co-worker, Mya

Taylor, a.k.a. my competition for the biggest ad account this side of the Atlantic.

Our client wants a wedding expert so I'm suddenly fake-engaged to a woman who hates me AND would gladly put my balls in her purse. But when I find out she's never taken a trip to O-town, we make a little wager.

Not only will I win the client, but I'll prove to her that multiples are NOT a myth. We work together all day and fight between the sheets all night. But at the end of the day, it's still a competition.

May the best man win.

BEG ME is a frenemies to lovers, completely inappropriate romantic comedy. Side effects may include clutching your pearls and laughing until you almost choke.

Download BEG ME now
at minxmalone.com/begme

Excerpt of *Beg Me* © 2018 M. Malone

MILO

Time to get our game faces on.

As we approach the table, everyone stands, and the introductions are made all around. Maybe it's because I'm watching Mr. Lavin so closely that I see how his eyes follow Mya after she shakes his hand and then walks around the table to greet the other members of his team. She knows all of their names, as do I. Then she takes a seat right next to me.

Before I can even sit down, James is already ordering a scotch from the waitress. Then I see why.

Elizabeth is sitting two tables away.

She raises her glass of wine in our direction. I turn to see James give a begrudging wave. I'm not sure if anyone else has noticed her yet, but she's already accomplished her goal. There's no way James can focus completely on the client tonight with his ex-wife sitting right in his line of vision.

Christ.

"Thank you all for traveling to meet with me. I've had this week scheduled with potential investors for months, so it's been helpful that you could come to me while I'm already in the States."

"When do you go back to Italy?" Wallace asks. "I follow you on Instagram. You guys, his page is *lit*. Fast cars, beautiful clothes. You're living the dream, man." He sighs before digging into his salad course enthusiastically.

Andre just laughs. "Thank you. This is our goal, to be as the kids say, *fire*. Why is all of the American slang centered around temperature, I wonder? It used to be that things were *cool*, now they're *hot, fire, bomb* or *lit*. Fascinating. I have an entire team of people who study the social media trends."

James looks like he has no idea what is happening. But I strongly suspect that Wallace in his own unique, bumbling way has just broken the ice for us.

Well, if he's broken the ice, I might as well jump in first. "Mirage employs a lot of talented young designers. It's why our ad campaigns are so on trend. We combine years of experience in understanding what makes people buy with the fresh perspective of different generations."

Mya grins over at me. "Wallace is on Milo's team. He's been with us for almost a year now and graduated from

Columbia with honors. He's also an amateur photographer and is pretty popular on Instagram, too."

I glance over at her. *He is?* How does she know all that? Maybe there is something to paying attention in those bullshit icebreaker sessions at work after all.

Wallace looks shocked, too. "My account has nowhere near the numbers some of my friends have, but I just passed ten thousand."

Mr. Lavin actually looks impressed. "That's quite an accomplishment, especially for a hobbyist." He clears his throat. "I'm happy to meet with you all in person after hearing about you from Mr. Lawson."

James gives him a tight smile. "I'm extremely proud of my team."

"It shows," Andre replies.

Dinner proceeds with the typical pleasantries. Wallace looks a little confused, but I can only pray the kid can hold his tongue. With these types of clients, you never rush right into business. You need to woo them, almost like a woman you're trying to convince to come back to your place after dinner. She's not just going to come with you if you ask within the first ten minutes. She needs you to show her that you're worth her time. Are you going to savor her the same way you do the ten-inch porterhouse on your plate? Or will you rush through the act like a kid scarfing down an ice cream cone?

I can't imagine a man like Andre Lavin scarfing anything. He needs to see that we're not only the best team to take over his marketing but also that we're people he can work with.

We need him to *like* us.

As the waitress is clearing the entrees, Andre looks around the table with satisfaction. "Perhaps it is old-fashioned, but I care to meet with any agencies that work on our marketing directly. It's important that the people crafting our image understand what we're about here at Lavin Fashions."

Everyone instantly ceases their side conversations and pays attention. Now we're getting to the good stuff. The reason we're all here.

"What is your vision of Lavin Fashions, Mr. Lavin?" Mya asks. "I've read the official company mission statement, but I would love to hear it from you."

"Please, call me Andre."

The way he's looking at her makes it seem like he just wants to hear her say his name. My hand sitting on top of the table curls into a fist. It's unsettling that this bothers me. He's just a client, throwing a little charm at the pretty ad executive. I've seen it plenty of times, and I've had my fair share of clients, male and female, attempt to flirt with me.

None of those made me want to growl in frustration. Or made me worry that Mya might actually want to flirt back.

"It's much more than just the clothes," Andre begins after a brief pause. "Our brand creates the garments that become part of people's memories. And for our newest venture, we're looking for a partner that understands the importance of family, friendship, love."

The woman sitting next to him sniffs. *Cristiane Laveque.* From my research on the Lavin team, I know that she's a top designer for Lavin Fashions.

"Apologies, but this is not a strength of American companies, we have found. So few understand *l'amore.*" She shakes her head ruefully as if the vulgar ways of the American market are just too much.

Mentally, I'm rolling my eyes, but this could be a real obstacle to winning their business. If they think that we're not cultured enough, it will be difficult to change that opinion. Granted, Mirage does plenty of "American" commercials and brands, but it's not like we're all racecars and beer. We have plenty of upper-echelon brands in the jewelry, hotel and entertainment industries.

"I believe Mirage can handle anything. We have such a diverse workforce that all of our clients find someone they can relate to. We also have more women in leadership roles than many of our competitors."

Maybe that'll calm her fears that we don't get *l'amore*. Mya in particular handles a lot of brands that cater to women, including a high-profile lingerie line.

Andre sits back in his chair and seems to be considering her words. "I must admit we've been approached by other firms that are run by people who are married. They understand what brides want."

James sits up straighter. "So, it is a bridal line?"

Andre laughs lightly. "Yes, the rumors are true. Lavin Fashions will introduce a new line called Lavin Bridal next year. It will be a separate division of the company which is why I'm meeting with investors. I didn't want word to get out until it was all finalized."

James looks like he's going to be sick. This is why Elizabeth has been so smug. She must have heard the Lavin group wanted someone who has been through the process of planning a wedding. Just another way for her to rub her recent marriage in James's face.

"I'm sure all the women on our team have mentally planned their dream wedding, even if they aren't married." I send a panicked glance at Mya.

This would be a really good fucking time for her to pipe in with some story of how she's been dreaming of her wedding dress since she was a little girl.

Unfortunately, Andre seems to be following my line of thought because he turns directly to Mya, too. "If you were planning a wedding, for example," he says, "wouldn't you want a wedding planner who was married?"

Mya pauses with her water glass halfway to her mouth. "Well, yes. I suppose I would."

James just blinks. Wallace pauses mid-chew with a piece of iceberg lettuce hanging from his lip. The whole table seems stunned into silence. She didn't mean to say that, and everyone can see it on her face. But in a rare, caught-off-guard moment, Mya has done the unforgivable.

She's been honest.

An awkward silence descends over the table. James takes another gulp from his scotch. Across from me, members of the Lavin team exchange significant glances before taking an interest in their plates. Worst of all, Andre Lavin just looks amused.

While Mya looks devastated.

You know how sometimes you can look back and identify the precise moment you fucked up? Well, later tonight I'm sure I'll be remembering the exact second I pushed us all off the cliff together.

"I agree," I state loudly.

James chokes slightly, and Wallace pounds him on the back. I ignore his panicked look and keep my eyes on Mr. Lavin.

"I agree with Mya," I repeat in case anyone at the table missed it the first time I pushed my career in front of a bus. "Having a married wedding planner would be great. Although I'd be more concerned about the people actually doing the work. That's really what sets Mirage apart."

By now, everyone is staring at me, especially James, probably wondering where the hell I'm going with this.

Mya, however, is watching me with a small, tremulous smile on her face. Like she can't believe that I'm backing her up right now. And damn if that smile isn't what does me in. Because I don't just bet on distracting Mr. Lavin; I double down and take it all the way to the bank.

"Mirage is really the best fit for anything to do with weddings. After all, it's the only agency I know with two team leads that are in love and engaged to be married." I turn to Mya and whisper, "Just go with it."

Then I tilt my head slightly and brush my lips over hers.

MYA

Everyone is staring. I can feel the heat of their eyes on the side of my face. But even that isn't enough to take me out of this moment. This sweet, thrilling moment. My eyes drift closed, and the world falls away.

Milo is kissing me.

If you'd asked me just an hour ago what kind of kisser I thought Milo would be, I'd have said aggressive. He's all about going all-in and getting to the finish line. I would have assumed that he wouldn't care much about the process but rather only about the end game.

I would have been completely and utterly wrong.

His lips are soft, and he feathers them over mine gently, barely touching me. The result is a whispery soft touch that sends chills up and down my spine. Then he lays his mouth over mine and kisses me properly, his tongue brushing softly against mine.

After what feels like several hours but is probably only several seconds, he pulls back. But he doesn't just stop. No, Milo can't do anything simply, not even shocking me to my core with a kiss. Because right after he pulls away, he does this soft little nuzzle, rubbing his nose back and forth against mine.

Why is that my kryptonite? That completely unnecessary little snuggle just takes all the indignation I was building up to and scatters it into the wind. Along with all rational thought.

A throat clears and it's like jumping into an ice bath. If we'd been standing, we'd have probably sprung apart, but instead I grope the table blindly until my hand connects with my water glass. The icy liquid cools my throat but not my lust.

What the hell was that?

Everyone at the table is still eating and talking softly amongst themselves, almost like the last thirty seconds didn't just change the rotational orbit of the planet. Isn't it funny how a certain event can knock you off your feet but seems to have no effect on anyone else? It's like experiencing an earthquake while everyone around you goes on with their lives unaware. Well, everyone isn't unaware. Andre Lavin is watching us carefully.

So is James.

Oh shit.

This is where I should speak up. Tell Mr. Lavin that I cannot wait to see his newest designs, that women everywhere are going to be clamoring for the chance to wear one of his dresses. But I can't because my mind is still muddled, and I can still feel the imprint of Milo's lips against mine.

"You make an interesting point, Mr. Hamilton. Being married is one thing, but to have a couple who are currently planning a wedding designing my campaign would be ideal." Mr. Lavin nods in satisfaction. "I had a good feeling about this firm, but I can see that your reputation is accurate. Professional, innovative and discreet. Exactly what I need."

James looks slightly dazed, the same expression you might wear after you narrowly miss being hit by a cab. He looks between me and Milo and then back to Mr. Lavin, but nothing comes out of his mouth.

Once again, Wallace comes to the rescue. "You can't go wrong with those two in charge, if you're looking for discretion. They've been dating in secret for ages and nobody knew except for me. I mean, I could tell. He stares at her ass whenever she walks away."

The water I just sipped comes back up my nose.

Milo hands me a napkin without missing a beat. "Thank you, Wallace. So, Mr. Lavin, tell us about your vision for Lavin Bridal in particular."

And so it goes. Milo manages to carry the conversation all the way through the dessert course and then through coffee. Personally, I've never understood the practice of drinking coffee after dessert, but when the waitress comes around, I order some anyway. Maybe the extra caffeine will wake me the hell up.

But I still feel like I'm sleepwalking as James bids the members of the Lavin team goodnight and they promise to be in touch. Wallace is the first to scamper off, probably to go post the selfie he took with Mr. Lavin to Instagram. The thought makes me chuckle, but my throat instantly turns to sandpaper when James approaches.

This entire time, Milo and I have been sitting in silence. I couldn't take the chance of asking any questions where the Lavin team might overhear. But now I wish I'd thought to text him or something so I'd know how we're handling this.

But James doesn't look upset at all. He's practically glowing. It could be all the scotch, but either way, he looks thrilled.

"You two, ah, I should have known. You've done an amazing job keeping your relationship out of the office. Good work. Knew I could count on you." He claps Milo on the shoulder and gifts me with a wide, loopy grin.

Even if I knew what to say to him right now, I don't think I'd have the heart to wipe that smile off his face. Tomorrow is soon enough for him to realize that we've screwed up this deal. Maybe a good night's sleep will make him more lenient when he's deciding whether to fire us.

Milo pulls out my chair for me as I stand, and I follow wordlessly as we leave the restaurant. It's a Thursday night, but as we walk back through the casino to reach the elevators to the rooms, there are so many people out you'd never think it was a weekday. Time seems to move differently here. I notice an older lady with a purple fanny pack methodically feeding coins into a slot machine. She looks like she's been at it for a while. Maybe I should just stay down here, living off the free drinks and the adrenaline of gambling. It would probably be better than what's waiting for me when we get back to DC.

I'm so deep in my thoughts that I'm not paying attention when we get on the elevator. It's only when it stops that I realize we didn't push the button for my floor. But Milo loops his arm around my waist and guides me out of the elevator anyway.

"But my room—"

"Not here," he murmurs in my ear. The deep rumble of his voice so close sends a shiver down my spine. "Some of the Lavin team are on this floor. Wait until we get inside."

"Inside what?" Belatedly, I realize he means inside his room. He has his key card out and the door open before I can say, *No way in hell.*

The door slams shut behind us, and all the things I was getting ready to say get stuck in my throat.

Trying to gather my thoughts, I look around the room. The layout is the same as the one I was given, TV, big window directly across from the door, except he has a king-size bed instead of two doubles. Behind him, there are several dress shirts scattered on the bed, and the covers are all tangled, like he took a nap before coming down to dinner. Just like that I have a mental image of Milo naked in those sheets, and being alone with him in this room seems like a *very* bad idea.

Completely at ease with the idea of the two of us being alone, he shrugs out of his suit jacket and loosens his tie. I'm instantly distracted by the small patch of skin revealed at the top of his shirt where it's unbuttoned. "I know you must have a million questions," he says finally.

But I don't. Truthfully, I only have one.

"What the hell just happened?"

Download BEG ME now
at minxmalone.com/begme

Also by M. Malone

Mess with Me (Romantic Comedy)

BEG ME (Milo & Mya)

My rooster is on strike. Yeah, I can't believe it either. But he'll only crow for one woman. Spoiler Alert *she hates me*

ASK ME (Andre & Casey)

Am I arrogant? Maybe. Do women still want me? Abso-F'ing-lutely. Then I meet the one woman who isn't impressed.

NEED ME (Vin & Ariana)

Crazy sh*t every day keeps relationships away. Except this guy who just *keeps* showing up. And if I'm not careful, I might get used to needing someone.

WANT ME (Law & Anya)

No strings. Sounds good, right? But if I'm not her boyfriend the position is open for someone else.

*** Join my VIP list for FREE books ***

newsletter.mmalonebooks.com

The Alexanders

One More Day : "Good girl" Ridley has always attracted bad guys. Now she's on the run and has nowhere to hide. So when Jackson Alexander mistakes her for her twin, for once she decides to do the "wrong" thing.

The Things I Do for You : Nicholas Alexander finally has something his dream girl needs. He'll give Raina a baby if she gives him what he wants. *Her*.

All I Want: The only thing Kay wants is for Elliott Alexander to stop treating her like she's invisible. But a car accident forces her to reach out to the only man she trusts to save her.

All I Need is You : When the man she loves leaves town after their steamy kiss, Kaylee Wilhelm is done. But when she's targeted by a stalker, Eli is the only one who can protect her.

Just One Thing : Scientist Bennett Alexander is a bona fide genius but he still needs a dating tutor to "get the girl". What could go wrong? Other than falling for his teacher, of course!

The Simmons

Make Him Mine : When he's not pretending she's invisible, Trent sees Mara Simmons as the little sister he never had. But she finally has a plan to get him exactly where he should be. *In her bed*.

Make Me Feel : Matt Simmons is over Army doctors poking him until he sees his physical therapist is h-o-t. All Penny wants is to put down roots which means NO military men. And Sgt. Sexy isn't going to change her mind.

Make Her Stay : Mara has always known Trent Townsend is *The One*. But when his frequent business trips turn out to have *nothing* to do with business, she discovers the man she loves just might be a stranger.

Bad Business (The Kingsleys)

Bad King: My parents just put a gold diggers target on my back. But if all they want is a wedding, I can do that. I'll find the fiancee of their nightmares. *Who Wants to Marry a Billionaire? Must be completely inappropriate.*

Bad Blood : I'd do anything for my best friend's little sister. Until she asks for the one thing I can't give. One night. No rules. ***RITA® Award Winner!***

Blue-Collar Billionaires

Billions from the deadbeat dad they never knew sounds pretty sweet. Until they find out what he really wants.

Tank / Finn / Gabe / Zack / Luke

- Romantic Suspense -

(Co-authored with Nana Malone)

- The Shameless Trilogy
- The Force Duet
- The Deep Duet
- The Sin Duet
- The Brazen Duet

- Paranormal Romance -

Nathan's Heart

The Brotherhood of Bandits

About the Author

M. Malone is a RITA® Award winner and a NYT & USA Today Bestselling author of completely inappropriate romantic comedy. She spends most days wearing Wonder Woman leggings while she plays with her imaginary friends.

She lives with her husband and their two sons in the picturesque mountains of Northern Virginia even though she is afraid of insects, birds, butterflies and other humans.

She also holds a Master's degree in Business from a prestigious college that would no doubt be scandalized at how she's using her expensive education.

facebook.com/minxmalone

twitter.com/minxmalone

instagram.com/minxmalone

bookbub.com/authors/m-malone

9 781938 789489